WET DREAMS ON LOCKDOWN

The Male C.O

TAMYRA GRIFFIN

URBAN AINT DEAD

URBAN AINT DEAD PRESENTS

Wet Dreams On Lockdown:
The Male C.O

By Tamyra Griffin

URBAN AINT DEAD

P.O Box 448
Maybrook, NY 12543

preparation of this book, the publisher and the author assume no responsibility for errors or omissions. Neither is any liability assumed for damages resulting from the use of the information contained herein. This is a work of fiction. Names, characters, places, and incidents are either the product of the author's imagination or are used fictitiously. Any resemblance to actual events, locales, or persons living or dead is entirely coincidental.

Contact Author on FB: Tamyra Griffin / IG: @authortamyragriffin

Contact Publisher at www.urbanaintdead.com

Email: urbanaintdead@gmail.com

ISBN: 979-8-9902387-2-5

CONTENTS

SOUNDTRACKS

Scan the QR Code below to listen to the Soundtracks/Singles
of some of your favorite U.A.D titles:

Don't have Spotify or Apple Music?
No Sweat!
Visit your choice streaming platform and search URBAN
AINT DEAD.

Currently on lock serving a bid?
JPay, iHeartRadio, WHATEVER!
We got you covered.

Simply log into your facility's kiosk or tablet, go to music and
search URBAN AINT DEAD.

URBAN AINT DEAD

Like & Follow us on social media:
FB - URBAN AINT DEAD
IG: @urbanaintdead
Tik Tok - @urbanaintdead

SUBMISSIONS

Submit the first three chapters of your completed manuscript to urbanaintdead@gmail.com, subject line: Your book's title. The manuscript must be in a .doc file and sent as an attachment. The document should be in Times New Roman, double-spaced, and in size 12 font. Also, provide your synopsis and full contact information. If sending multiple submissions, they must each be in a separate email. Have a story but no way to submit it electronically? You can still submit to URBAN AINT DEAD. Send in the first three chapters, written or typed, of your completed manuscript to:

URBAN AINT DEAD
P.O Box 448
Maybrook, NY 12543

DO NOT send original manuscript. Must be a duplicate.
Provide your synopsis and a cover letter containing your full contact information.
Thanks for considering URBAN AINT DEAD.

Chapter 1

"Silence!" Officer Lewis barked. "This shit here ain't no sorority house. This is a prison! Single file line, inmates…and welcome home," he added with a smirk as he walked the line of ladies that had just arrived.

I stood there and shook my head as I watched this asshole act like he owned the prison – which was a daily routine. He wasn't the only asshole on staff though. Me, on the other hand, I lived by the motto – *do your eight and skate*. However, I didn't treat the inmates the way other COs did. Yeah, they were in prison for committing a crime, but it didn't make them any less human. I mean, I wasn't trying to be the cell block savior, but I did my job the way it was supposed to be done.

Today was Friday – which was dubbed New Arrival Day at Garden State Women's Correctional Facility. Most people looked forward to this because it ended the week, but for me, it was my least favorite day. Some of the women had never been to prison, so there were all kinds of tears, theatrics, passing out. You name it, it's happened. The existing inmates showed their asses as well. You would think some of them were niggas the way they acted as they sized up the "fresh meat' being brought in. On both ends of the spectrum, there was a lot of unnecessary drama and bullshit to close out the week. TGIF my ass.

After the new arrivals were processed in, searched, and given their gear, I stood at the entry of the tier with my counter, making sure everybody was accounted for. I only paid attention to 'em long enough to make sure my count was right at this point in the process. Although, you couldn't help but take notice of some of the women that came in. Of course, you could pick out the junkies right away. Then there were the privileged, scared white women that got caught up in some white-collar bullshit – and my least favorite, the repeat offend-ers. They were my least favorite – because they always felt the need to test your gangsta, and most times ended in the need to get physical.

This particular day, I happened to look up at one inmate when her feet didn't move, and I heard kissing noises. When I looked up at the stringy-haired white woman, she smiled, revealing a mouth full of brown-ish colored, rotten teeth.

"When I get all settled in, come find me. I'd love to taste

your chocolate stick," she said flirtatiously before licking her lips with a white-coated tongue.

"Move your ass along before I write your ass up." I spat, offended at just the thought of my dick anywhere near her trash mouth. "I said **move**…inmate!"

"If you change your mind…I ain't going nowhere," she returned with a wink before taking her ass on her way.

Officer Lewis stood a few feet away from me, briefly laughing at the exchange before he went back to talking his shit to the women as they walked by. I continued my count until I heard him say, "Well damn, beautiful. Looks like you're in the wrong place. What's your name, sexy?" he flirted, eyeing the woman he was lusting over, who I couldn't see clearly.

"Inmate number 9237560," she replied with a bit of spunk before taking a step forward with the rest of the line.

"Aiight then. I'll give ya bougie ass a few days before you're begging to be in daddy's good graces," he spat. "Get ya ass on then."

When the woman finally came into view, I could see the reasoning behind his initial reaction. She was indeed beautiful. She wasn't quite plus size, but she was thicker than a Snicker in all the right places. Her long, naturally curly, red-ish colored hair was pulled up into a messy bun, and even under the poor prison lighting, her skin glowed. Sexy pouty lips, almond eyes, and a cute button nose were perfectly placed – making her one of the most beautiful women I'd ever seen. It also made me wonder what a woman like her was doing in a place like this – but you could never judge a book by its cover. When she reached the front of the line, I couldn't help but look into her eyes. I could see more hurt than I saw fear, along with a hint of sadness. Those things alone made me want to know more about her, but that may never happen. After all, fraternizing with inmates was strictly forbidden – although other COs found ways around that.

I gave her a polite nod and she lowered her eyes before stepping through the door to line up behind the other ladies that were waiting to be shown to their new place of residence.

"Man! Did you see the bubble on the back of that bougie bitch?!" Lewis perked. "I bet that thang is beautiful bent over – all spread out for the spankin'," he added as he rubbed his hands together.

"I thought you had a girl?" I asked, annoyed with his ignorance.

"*Girls*, my nigga. These hoes are like Lay's potato chips. You can't have just one," he returned. "You get off your boy scout bullshit, you could have you a few biddies up in here; and it's the best kind of pussy to get. They test these hoes, so you know which ones are clean and which ones not. That right there is called *free fuckin'*."

"I think you do enough free fuckin' for the both of us." I returned with a smirk. That nigga got on my last damn nerve at times – mostly on Fridays.

"Shiiiiid. I can never get enough of free, disease-free

pussy. You buggin', and making me question ya sexuality, my nigga."

"Don't worry about me. I'm good."

"Aiight. Well, if you change your mind…holla at ya boy."

Even away from the prison, I couldn't get my mind off of the mysterious beauty I locked eyes with. I couldn't concentrate on the game of *Madden* I was playing because I needed to know more about her. I logged into the Department of Corrections website to do a little research.

"Natifah Foxworth," escaped aloud from my mouth when her mugshot and information popped up on my screen.

Even in her mugshot, she was beautiful. Getting over the distraction of her looks, I looked down at the charges that had landed her at Garden State. Only one charge was listed, and it was a conspiracy charge. Wanting to know more information than the website offered, Google was my next stop. After punching in her name and county, a couple of news articles popped up on her. I sipped my ice cold Modelo as I began to read the first article on her after glancing briefly at the picture of her leaving the courthouse.

"Classic fuck boy scenario." I said aloud as I read the article.

From what I gathered after reading the first article, her man was a piece of shit drug dealer who left her in the dark about his bullshit. It also said that she was the owner of her own nail salon and beauty supply store, had been an honor student and homecoming queen, and graduated salutatorian.

She was a bonified good girl. Towards the end of the article, it mentioned her man was sentenced to ten years, while she received sixteen months due to having no criminal background. Intrigued and wanting to know more about Ms. Foxworth, I surfed Google a little bit more. There were pictures of her at her salon's grand opening and Facebook photos of her at different events and charity functions. This woman seemed to be everything a man could ask for in his queen; but this queen was behind bars unfortunately, and off limits to me. Although that was the reality of the situation, I felt the need to get to know her better. For the first time in a long time, I was looking forward to Monday.

MONDAY WAS mess hall duty day for me, which I hated, but today it was welcomed. The tier Ms. Foxworth was housed in wasn't part of my detail, so it was my opportunity to get a glimpse of or even talk to her today. I low key looked around for her while keeping an eye on the other inmates. When she walked into the mess hall, I had to stop myself from staring. She'd survived the weekend and didn't appear to have a scratch on her from what I could see as I watched her walk over to the chow line. Once she got her tray, which she looked at and rolled her eyes, she walked past me with a book tucked under her arm towards an empty table. Even after washing with the cheap prison issued soap, she left a waft of jasmine and vanilla when she passed. After taking a seat, she almost caused my eyes to bulge from their sockets when she bowed her head to pray.

"Look at the princess over there," an inmate everyone called Big Meesh said.

Big Meesh was the resident bully, lesbian rapist, snitch, etc. If it was dirt to be done, Big Meesh had her hands in it. She got away with it due to an arrangement she had with certain staffers, so she acted as if she ran the joint.

"The Lord can't save you up in here, prom queen. Having the right friends can help you though." Big Meesh offered as she lustfully eyed her before licking her lips. "What's your name, pretty?" she asked when she got no reaction.

Ms. Foxworth nibbled cutely on a piece of bread, probably the only edible thing on the tray, and kept her nose in her book. I stood watch as Big Meesh got up front her seat, walked over, and stood behind her. Faster than I could blink, Big Meesh had grabbed a handful of Ms. Foxworth's beautiful hair and pulled her head back until she was almost looking at her. I was prepared to step in for the save, since Big Meesh had some size on her and would no doubt do her dirty; but as I took my first step towards them, Ms. Foxworth had already taken action. There was no fear in her eyes as she bent her arm and power thrusted her elbow in to Meesh's midsection, causing her to let go of her hair and double over in pain.

"Don't fuck with me and we won't have no problems."

Ms. Foxworth said in a sweet voice, but her tone let you know she played no games.

"I'mma kill you, bitch!" Big Meesh roared before standing straight and rushing towards her.

Side-stepping Meesh's outstretched arms, Foxworth stuck out her foot, tripping Meesh and sending her to the floor. The commotion in the mess hall was so loud from the other inmates that you could hardly hear the alarm blaring, alerting other officers of the incident. Seeing Big Meesh getting up off the floor and some of her flunkies surrounding Foxworth, I rushed over just as a punch was thrown and connected with her face. Ms. Foxworth paused a moment to shake the lick off before coming back with an uppercut of her own that sent another flunkie to the floor.

"Damn!" I exclaimed at the Mortal Kombat style punch before I had to regroup and be professional. "That's enough, inmate! Break this shit up! Back up! Now!" I barked as Big Meesh and her minions circled like sharks.

I grabbed Foxworth by the arm, placing myself between her and her attackers as I waved another officer for Meesh and her crew. When they arrived, I turned my attention back to Inmate Foxworth.

"Move, inmate!" I said sternly but couldn't bring myself to speak as harshly to her as I had the other inmates.

She didn't resist, but she had one request.

"Could you please make sure I get my book back?" she asked sweetly.

I waited until we were away from the commotion and ears of the other officers before I spoke.

"Are you okay?" I asked with concern in my voice.

"I'm fine. Thanks," was all she offered.

"You don't look like you belong in here, so I'm gonna give you a few words of advice. You see Big Meesh or any of her flunkies coming, you might wanna go the other way for a while. Either that or keep delivering those super punches." I said softly.

That got a cute little chuckle out of her before she glanced my way.

"Thanks for the heads up, officer."

"Jabril. Officer Pratt formally."

"Natifah Foxworth."

"Nice to meet you Foxworth."

"Where are you taking me?"

"To solitary – until the warden is ready to see you."

"Solitary? For defending myself?"

"It won't be for long after I make my report. I tell you what, if the process takes too long, I'll come by to check on you."

"You'd do that?"

"I got you."

It wasn't until the next day that I was sent to solitary to retrieve Inmate Foxworth, and I couldn't believe she was kept in there overnight. When I opened the door, she shielded her eyes from the bright hallway lights as she stood.

"Good morning," she said softly after clearing her throat. "It is morning, isn't it?"

"It is." I replied and stepped into the doorway. "Here, sip this before I put the cuffs on you. It's just spring water."

"Oh God, thank you," she said as she took the small flask I offered.

I didn't believe in all that electricity and sparks flowing through your body crap – until her fingers grazed mine. She had the softest skin I'd ever felt, and just that simple touch sent currents through me. I stole a glance at her as she finished the water, placed the cap back on the flask, and handed it to me.

"Thank you again," she said in that sweet voice. "Where to now?"

"To see the warden, then to your bunk. Your belongings are already there, and I put your book in there for you."

"Are all COs as nice as you?" she asked seriously.

"Not even – unless they want something from you. If you catch my meaning, and before you ask, that's not what this is. I'm one of the rare ones who doesn't feel like you should be treated like an animal since you're in a cage. Just keep your eyes and ears open, and your neck on swivel at all times. You never know which direction the bullshit is gonna come from."

"I appreciate you. Thanks again."

"Thank me by staying outta trouble and staying safe." I returned and offered a slight smile. "Let's move."

Touching the silky-smooth skin on her arm had the same

effect on me that it had the day before. This woman had me ready to risk it all. I had to tell myself to pump my brakes – getting this excited over an inmate. I wanted to know more about the mysterious Ms. Natifah Foxworth, but seeing the effect she already had on me, that may not be such a good idea. Especially if I want to stay employed.

Chapter 2

For the remainder of the week, I hadn't been able to lay eyes on Inmate Foxworth. To say I was in my feelings, was an understatement. By Friday morning, I had come to grips with the fact that I wasn't going to see her again this week. It was new arrival day, and then after that, I was on patrol in the library for the rest of my shift. The only silver lining to that was, I was gonna be able to take a nap.

"Fresh fish Friday! My favorite day of the week." Officer Lewis' pervert ass beamed as he stood across from me rubbing his hands together, licking his lips.

"How does someone losing their freedom bring you so much joy?" I asked with a scowl.

"The fuck I care about that shit," he spat. "They did what they did to get here, not me. I benefit because these prison hoes are freaks! And no pussy like prison pussy. You need to get off all your kumbaya bullshit and get you some. Maybe that's what's wrong with ya ass. Ya balls too tight."

"My balls ain't none of ya damn business." I spat.

"I'm just saying, dawg," he said with a shrug of his shoulders as the alarm sounded, alerting us to the opening of the gate.

Once the short line of new inmates was lined up and Lewis finished with his usual bullshit, I moved to the entry door with my counter. He was acting like it was Friday night at the club and he was scouting pussy rather than acting like he was at work – in a women's prison!

AFTER SCARFING down a chicken cheesesteak on my lunch break, the itis threatened to kick in as I made my way to the library. I had scoped out the perfect corner to nap in when this was part of my patrol, and I couldn't wait to get to it. As soon as I walked in to relieve the last officer, I began my rounds so I could get to my nap – which I needed bad at this point. As I got to the last row of books, which was also where I planned to nap, I got a real eye opener. Inmate Foxworth turned to look at me and gave me a slight smile before she went back to putting books back on the shelves.

"Nice to see you again – outside of solitary." I offered with a slight smile of my own.

"Nice to see you too. I wanted to thank you again. I really

appreciated it. Especially since I know you could've gotten in trouble," she said, softly.

"Certain situations warrant the sacrifice. I'm glad I could help. You didn't belong there anyway. And if you don't mind me saying, I don't think you belong here either." I said, unable to resist.

"I don't – but I do. I guess this is a hard lesson learned for allowing my heart to blind me from the things my mind showed me," she returned with a hint of sadness.

"I um… Do you mind if I-"

"You want the long or short version?" she asked, still slowly putting books on the shelf.

"It's your choice. I've got time," was my reply as I sat in the chair that I was supposed to be napping in.

"Okay. Well, my best friend is the general manager of an upscale hotel. There are a lot of parties and conventions there. Anyway, I was meeting her after her shift so we could go out, and I went inside. We're talking, and here comes this guy who was there for the party. I turned him down a couple of times when he asked for my number. The third time he asked, I gave it to him. Long story short, he was a wolf in sheep's clothing. He told me he owned a car detailing shop – which he did and served as a front for some other shit – but he turned out to be a piece of shit dealer. Unfortunately, that information didn't come to light for me until the police were kicking the door in. Interrogations, court dates, more interrogations, sentencing, and here I am. Learning my hard lesson," she finished, dropping her head slightly with a hint of sadness and tears in her eyes.

"I hope those tears aren't for him. He doesn't deserve them; and it sounds like he didn't deserve you."

"You're right, and no. I have no tears for him. Only feelings of disdain – and maybe a Floyd Mayweather combo if I ever got lucky enough to have the chance," she seethed.

"Oh, I saw that *Mortal Kombat* uppercut you sent home-girl to the floor with. If he was a smart man, I don't think he'd want any parts of that." I cracked and laughed lightly.

"You're right again," she returned with a beautiful closed-mouth smile as she moved a stray curl from her eye bash-fully. "Now as far as how smart he is, that remains ques-tionable."

"I probably shouldn't say this, but you seem really sweet, educated, cultured. Why would you date a man like that?"

"Unfortunately, the heart wants what the heart wants," she said sadly as she looked away. "Had I stuck to my guns and turned him down that third time, I wouldn't be here right now, but the devil's tongue is a cunning one."

"Now that's fact if I've never heard it." I agreed.

"Well, it was nice talking to you Officer Jabril Pratt. I better go finish up before the CO comes looking for me," she smiled at me again as she placed her hands on the book cart to push away.

"I wasn't looking for you, but I see you." I said – then wanted to slap my damn self for saying it. "I was actually looking for this spot to take a nap on the low, but talking to you was better."

"You seem like one of the good ones, Officer Pratt. Your wife should consider herself a lucky woman."

"She will be… when I find her – or she finds me."

"You might be one of the last black unicorns. Whatever you do, stay away from those cunning tongues. Don't let anything or anyone taint the goodness in you. There's a shortage of good people today," she stated.

I could tell from the way she spoke and the look in her eyes that she'd been hurt. Betrayed. I'd just met this woman, but something in me wanted to take her in my arms and promise her I'd take all her pain away. There was just *something* about her energy that sucked you in, and it wasn't intentional.

"Only if you do the same."

"Absolutely. Goodness…that's what makes life worth living," she returned as she smiled. "You go ahead and get a cat nap in. I'm gonna put the rest of these books away, but I'll cover you."

"I appreciate that, Foxworth."

"You can call me Natifah…if you want," she said shyly before dropping her eyes.

"I appreciate you…Natifah."

Needless to say, the dream that I had while napping was a sweet one indeed. Starring the one and only Ms. Natifah Foxworth. The woman I couldn't get off my mind.

Almost every CO on staff hated library detail. Therefore, they stick the new kid on the block with it as soon as they get the chance. So, I had to hide my excitement when I saw that's where I was scheduled to be stationed the rest of the week. Especially after I did my research and saw that's where Inmate Foxworth – or rather Natifah – was work detail. Just for good measure, I sighed before grabbing my gear and heading to the library – making sure I flipped a laughing Lewis the bird. I swear I don't know why I talk to him sometimes.

When I walked into the library, there were only two inmates inside. Natifah was helping the older of the two with some research she was doing as I made my way to the hub. When she looked up and we locked eyes, she gave me a bash smile before moving a stray hair and focusing her attention back on the inmate. After logging into the system and doing some paperwork, I headed back out to the library to make my rounds. When I came out, she was no longer at the table with the older inmate, and three more had come in.

"Get what you need and have a seat, ladies," I said to them since they were a little too noisy for my liking.

The ladies complied, and I commenced to walking up and down the aisles. When I got to the end of the third row and was rounding the fourth, I walked right into Inmate Foxworth, knocking some books from her hand.

"I'm so sorry, Officer Pratt," she rushed out and moved to get the books.

"No, let me. I should've been paying more attention." I

said as I squatted to gather the books. "Where are you taking them?"

"Right over here," she replied and pointed before leading the way. "Thank you," she added as she took the books to place on her cart.

"Is it stupid to ask how you're doing today?" I asked.

"It's not. A day in here is still…a day. I'm doing okay. Thanks for asking. How about you?" she asked as she began placing the books on the shelf.

I was a little delayed in my response, watching her put the books on the shelves. Not one book was out of place when she moved from the section she worked in. It was almost OCD-ish but also cute.

"Do you do every shelf like this?" I questioned instead of answering her question.

"Of course. I don't know… I kinda have a thing about organization, and I'm a little bit of a neat freak," she answered and chuckled.

"Can I ask what you did for a living – before coming here?"

"I own a nail salon and beauty supply. I opened the nail salon first. Grew that baby, and when the space next door became available, I hopped on that too. Asians have the beauty supply chain on lock, so I figured I'd get in on the action. Maybe give the hood an alternative place to shop for what they need."

"Wow. That's… impressive." I said with a nod, genuinely

impressed. Also confirming my suspicion that she didn't belong here.

"Thank you. I worked my ass off, but it was all worth the sacrifice."

"Let me know if I'm being nosey, but what will you do when you get out?" I asked before adding, "Whenever that may be." Even though we all know that I already know when.

"Well, thank God I have a solid team and support system. Between my best friend and my sister, they'll take care of my business for the sixteen months I'm here. I owned my businesses before I met the asshole, so they still belong to me. Hopefully, if everything goes well with my appeal, I'll be outta here sooner than that."

"I hope that goes well for you, Natifah."

"Well, when you do get outta here, you get a mani and pedi on the house," she said as she slightly touched my fingers that hung over her cart. "I owe you at least that."

"Will you be the one doing my feet?" I asked with a wide grin.

"That would be a no," was her reply before we shared a laugh. "I don't do feet, but the mani…I can hook you up."

"I'll take you up on that then." I returned with a smile. "I'll let you get back to work. I'm around if you need me."

"Thanks."

Although I could tell she wasn't totally comfortable, and not quite sure how to take me, Natifah and I talked throughout the rest of the day. By the time her shift was up I'd learned she had a thing for butterflies, her favorite color was fuchsia, she was an only child, and dreamed of one day going to Paris.

Talking to her was so soothing; and although I avoided sexual topics, she was unintentionally turning me on. I could've sworn at one point in the day she bit her lip while eyeballing me, until I turned in her direction, and it was the cutest shit ever. This woman woke all of my senses. *Damn! Why'd she had to be behind bars?* Maybe she'd turn out to really be a psycho and show her true colors, which would make it easy for me to be uninterested in her. Because at this point, I didn't know how much longer I'd be able to be around this woman without kissing her.

Chapter 3

had made a decision over the weekend that it was best if I no longer engaged in conversation with Natifah. I mean, Inmate Foxworth. I made the decision after a spank session – if you get my meaning – and called out her name. I knew then that she had taken up space in my head. So, I walked into the library that morning strictly business. I was gonna make my rounds and spend my time in the hub, away from Natifah. That went well until I ran into her during my walk around. Instead of her hair being pulled up into a messy bun, she wore her natural hair down today, which only added to her beauty. When she looked up briefly and smiled slightly at me before going back to her tasks, she weakened my resolve.

"Good morning, Officer Pratt," she said, not looking in my direction but feeling me staring at her.

"Good morning, Foxworth. Another day for the books, huh?" I cracked, and instantly regretted the corny joke, but she chuckled.

"I'll say."

"I'll say, even though I shouldn't… you're a beautiful woman. Even more so with your hair down." I offered with a smile.

"Actually, I um… I kinda hoped I saw you today and I wanted to do something different with it. You know, instead of you looking at me with the same ponytail," she admitted and blushed before her eyes widened and she straightened up, adding, "I apologize, officer. I'm not trying to step outta line or entice. I uh… I better get back to work."

She tossed a couple of books onto her cart and began pushing her cart in my direction, but at a rapid pace in order to speed past me. I stood in the corner where I usually napped, because the cameras didn't reach that corner. When she was almost next to me, something came over me that I couldn't control. Placing my hand atop hers, I removed it from the cart and pulled her towards me before kissing her passionately. At first, she was rigid, but once I deepened the kiss and her arms made their way to my shoulders, she offered me her tongue. Running my hands through her hair, we kissed like we were out in the free world and not hiding in the corner of the library inside of a women's prison. At the time though, neither of us realized that.

"I don't know what it is about you, but even when I'm not here, I can't get you off my mind." I admitted breathily as I looked into her beautiful brown eyes.

"I think about you too. I've never met a man like you… Officer Pratt. I just hope what I see is the real you and it's not about…"

"Unlike my co-worker, I'm not risking anything just to get my dick wet. Pardon the expression. That's not what I want. I want a genuine connection with a woman. It just so happens I feel a connection with you, and I'm struggling with that."

"So…what do we do?" she asked, wearing a look of fear and uncertainty on her face.

"I don't know…but can we start with you kissing me again?"

"I think that's a good place to start."

My hands began to roam her body as she sucked gently on my bottom lip before I felt her tongue touch mine again. With two handfuls of her soft ass, I lifted her until her legs wrapped around my waist. Pressing her back against the wall, I began licking and kissing on her neck, feeling my dick grow by the second when she left out a soft moan.

"God, I want you so bad right now," she whispered breathily, just as an alarm sounded loudly.

"Shit!" I seethed, quickly but gently letting her down.

I took a step to rush back to the hub to see what the fuck was going on but couldn't help to double back for one last quick kiss before I did. When she blushed and dropped her head, I had to will myself towards the chaos and away from her. Talk about a reality check to remind us of our circumstances. Damn!

A FEW DAYS had passed without me seeing Inmate Foxworth. Natifah. I loved saying her name. Anyway, I was assigned to the mess hall and intake for a few days after the alarm that interrupted what I hoped to continue with Natifah. When I saw that I was assigned to the library again, I couldn't hide the smile on my face.

When I walked into the library there was no sign of Natifah, so I went into the hub to settle into my tasks to get them out the way. Engrossed in an incident report, I didn't notice anyone in the doorway.

"Good morning, Officer Pratt." Natifah said softly, with a shimmer in her eyes. "Nice to see you."

"Good morning, Foxworth." I replied with a nod.

"I um… need to get into the storage closet. The old books I've been removing from the shelves need to be organized in there," she informed me.

"Give me just a minute and I'll be right there. Meet you at the door?"

"Okay. Thanks," she offered before blushing and walking away.

I grabbed the keys, talked shit to a couple of inmates that preferred sitting on the table instead of in chairs, and headed back to the storage room where Natifah was waiting. She stepped to the side to allow me to open the door.

"Let me help you with that." I offered as she attempted to grab and pull both heavy carts.

"Thank you. I guess I don't quite have the muscles I thought I had just yet," she cracked.

Once inside the room I watched as she went over to the back corner to make a space to work in. When she bent over to pick up an out of place book and I saw that beautiful, plump ass spread out before my eyes, letting the door close behind me, I walked up to her as she stood and turned around. Our eyes locked, and an animalistic lust came over me. Before I realized it, our lips were touching again. Her fingertips grazed my neck, sending jolts of electricity through my body. I had to have her. Backing her to the wall, my hands made their way beneath her shirt and up to her perky D cup breasts.

"Do you want me to stop?" I asked softly, hoping she'd say no.

"No...don't stop. Please," she moaned softly.

With the green light, I lifted her shirt and freed her breasts from her prison issued bra. Her gumdrop nipples made my mouth water, and I needed them between my lips. Natifah let out the sexiest moan as I worked my magic on the left nipple, then the right. Moving back to her lips, kissing hungrily again, her fingers toyed with the buckle of my belt before she got it unfastened. Placing my fingertips around the waist of her pants, I lowered them over her ass until she stood before me partially naked.

"Damn you're beautiful." I said on a strangled breath as I took her in before kissing her again.

Placing her leg on a shelf, she pulled me closer to her and began to massage my man, who was already oozing pre-cum. With one thrust, I filled her with all of my ten inches as our tongues danced – and I felt like I had died and gone to heaven. With her eyes closed and her lips parted, I admired the look of ecstasy on Natifah's face. Biting her bottom lip to keep from moaning out, her body lifted with each powerful thrust. I had never felt such a snug, wet pussy like hers. It felt like my dick was being massaged by velvet, and the struggle was real to keep from cummin'.

"You feel so…fuckin'…good, baby." I moaned because she damn sure did – but I needed to see that spread again.

Leaving her body, I turned her around and leaned her over a stack of boxes next to us. When I tell you that spread was even more beautiful bare, it was an understatement. It was so beautiful, I couldn't help but to spank that shit one more time before I filled her glistening, pink hole one more time; and when I did, the sensation made my toes twitch. When she began throwing it back at me, I felt my shit curl up in my work boots.

"What the…. fuuuuck!" I moaned through gritted teeth as I felt my nut rising.

"I'm cummin', baby. Shit!" Natifah whispered.

Unable to un-clinch my teeth for fear of growling out from the sensation as my climax approached, I filled my hands with baby soft ass cheeks as I watched my throbbing dick move in and out of her until it was covered with her creamy juices.

"Oh shit! Ooooooh shit!" I moaned loudly as my stroke became rigid.

Placing my hands on her waist, I plunged into her with purpose until I reluctantly removed my cream covered dick just in time to spill my seeds onto the floor as I panted. Taking a step back so she could stand, she turned around with flushed cheeks, looking freshly fucked.

"Officer Pratt, I…."

"Jabril." I corrected as I stepped towards her, pulled her close, and kissed her lips.

"Jabril… I um, I'm not one of those girls. What just happened, happened because I like you. I don't know if…."

"Natifah. It wouldn't have happened if I didn't feel the same. Like I told you, I ain't with the bullshit like these other clowns – and if one of 'em…"

"I know…I come to tell daddy," she cooed as she gently touched my face.

"I get to be daddy?" I asked, wearing a big ass grin.

"You can be. I'd like that," was her response before she fixed her clothes and kissed my lips.

"I'd like that too – but daddy gotta get back to his post so we don't get busted."

"Speaking of busted, do you have something we can use to clean up your…load?" she asked and laughed.

"Ha! You got jokes huh? Okay." I said and had to laugh before removing a handkerchief from my pocket. "I'm gonna go. I'll be back to check on you in a few."

"I'd like that."

I checked on her ass alright. Pussy so nice I had to do it twice and I was happy as hell that organizing the storage room wasn't a one-day project. Because I planned on sliding up in her silky pussy every chance that she gave me.

When I got home after work, I shed my uniform and headed towards the shower, which was my usual routine. As I moved to step foot into the shower, I was hesitant. If I breathed in deep enough, I could still catch a whiff of her essence, and all I wanted to do was marinate in it. Unfortunately, the smell of the prison overpowered her natural scent, so I proceeded to shower, and a nigga was sad that I had to wash her off of me. The realization that I was even thinking about sitting around funky, let me know that Natifah Foxworth had already sunk her claws into me without even realizing it. She was the flame, and I'm damn sure the moth…. gladly.

"OH…MY…. JABRIL!" Natifah softly moaned as she ran her hands over my head gently.

I swear it was the sexiest shit I'd ever heard. The fact that her pussy was the sweetest, juiciest pussy I'd ever tasted, along with her moans rooting me on, had me tasting her folds like we were in our private bedroom. My hands gently gripped her D cup breasts and caressed her nipple as I continued my assault on her clit until I felt her juices dripping from the corners of my mouth, onto my beard. But I wasn't done. Taking my pointer finger, I entered her dripping wet hole and found her g-spot, causing her to moan again. Flicking my tongue across her swollen nub skillfully, it took seconds to make her cum again.

"I need to feel you." I groaned before licking my lips, catching every last drop of her nectar.

Freeing my rock-hard dick, I helped her down from the pile of books so I could bend her over, but Natifah had other plans. Dropping slowly to her knees, she parted her lips and stuck out her long, thick tongue. Taking me into her mouth, she used her tongue to almost massage my dick as her warm spit began to coat my shaft.

"Ooooh fuck, babe." I groaned, already enjoying the feeling of her warm mouth on my dick.

She hummed even while I watched her head moving back and forth as she took almost all of my ten inches in without gagging. Running my fingers through her hair at first, I then gently grabbed a hand full of hair as I felt myself on the verge of cumming.

"Get up, beautiful." I softly instructed, helping her to her feet.

Pulling her to me, I kissed her deeply before turning her around and bending her over the pile of books. Just the sight of her slick, glistening opening had my dick dripping pre-cum as I filled her up.

"Damn you…feel so good," she whimpered.

I watched in awe as her pink pussy swallowed my dick, hugged it tight, and covered it with her creamy goodness. With every stroke it felt like her walls squeezed me tighter and tighter – until I had to clench my jaws to keep from growling like a wild animal. When she began to throw it back, I almost lost that battle.

"Mmmmm. Work your pussy, baby," she moaned in almost a whisper.

Feeling myself about to climax after she'd had yet another orgasm, I grabbed a cheek in each hand, giving me greater access. I began grinding deep into her, hitting her bottom until I couldn't take it anymore. I quickened my pace, also realizing we were pressed for time, and the light sound of skin slapping could be heard in the dusty room.

"Fuuuuck! I'm… I'm cumming, baby." I roared as I felt my toes begin to tingle before they curled up in my work boots. "Urrrrrrrrrrrrgh!"

Panting heavily, and unable to leave her body before I

came, I stood behind her with my hands on her hips, feeling my dick pulsing inside of her as I filled her with my seeds.

"That was…." I began but stopped to catch my breath.

"Amazing," she finished as she removed herself from my dick, since I was apparently stuck.

"Oh, I got something for you. Can't have you walking around the rest of your shift all juicy between the thighs." I said with a smile as I handed her a Ziploc bag with a couple of moist towelettes in there.

"Thank you," she said sweetly as she took the bag from my hand.

Removing a wipe from the bag, she took a step towards me to clean me off, but I protested.

"Nah. I wanna marinate in your sweet juices for a while." I said before kissing her softly. "Besides, there's PH balanced or some shit. Gynecologist recommended."

"Aren't you thoughtful?" she cooed before kissing me again, grazing my semi-flaccid dick.

"Aiight now. You gonna mess around and end up bent over again." I warned.

"I wouldn't mind that at all, but I think maybe you should make an appearance on camera. We can't have you getting in trouble. I would be devastated if I couldn't see you."

"You have a point, but I ain't going nowhere, ma." I sincerely promised before I realized it. "I'll let you get cleaned up and back to work. I gotta warn you though, I might need seconds when I come back to lock up."

"Say the word and it's yours."

"Shiiiit. I like the way that sounds." I groaned, stepping closer to her.

"Oh no you don't. Go ahead, let me at least get some work done," she coerced with a smile as she removed something from my beard.

"Oh…you did work alright." I cracked with a slight chuckle. "I'll check in on you in a bit."

As soon as the last inmate left the library, I locked the door behind her and made a b-line for Natifah. I found her outside of the storage closet, lining up the carts that needed to go inside to be stored away the next day. Unlocking the storage room door, I grabbed a cart for appearances to drag inside while Natifah grabbed another. As soon as the door closed behind her, I pinned her against the wall and kissed her deeply.

"What if…someone…. comes in?" she asked between kisses.

"I locked the door. We ain't got much time, but I needed to feel you again before I had to leave without you."

Freeing my rock-hard dick, I sat in the old wooden chair in the room and reached out for her hand. Taking one leg out of her prison-issued gear, Natifah straddled my lap, lowering herself slowly onto my dick. Offering her my tongue, she began to suck on it sensually as she began moving up and down slowly on my dick. Lifting her shirt and removing a breast from her bra, I sucked on her gumdrop nipples like they were my saving grace. With her eyes closed, biting her bottom lip sexily, I watched Natifah as she got lost in her zone. She let out this cute ass whimper as she came, which only made me wanna fuck her harder. The sound of my dick stirring her juices made it a challenge to hold onto my nut as I planned. So when I couldn't deal with the sweet torture anymore, I slammed her down on my dick and began thrusting into her, lifting her each time.

"J…Jabril! Daddy! Oh God!" she moaned out as I felt her juices coating my sack.

"I'm about to… cum, ma. Oh shit! Oooooooooou!" I moaned out, holding her close to my chest as I again filled her with my seeds.

"My God…where have you been all my life?" she asked breathily as she looked into my eyes.

"I could ask the same about you," was my response as I looked into her beautiful brown eyes. "As much as I hate to leave your body, you gotta dismount, babe."

"Tell me about it," she pouted as she moved.

"I hope you don't think…"

"No… It's okay. I was pouting because I know I have thinking about you all night to look forward to while I'm listening to my cell mate snore."

"I can't front, I do the same. Why you think I be wanting to marinate?" I cracked and gave her a smile. "I been meaning to ask. Any news on your appeal?"

"Actually, I just found out yesterday we have a court date coming up. So, I'm praying for a good outcome."

"I am too." I replied with a smile. "So…when you get out of here, do you think you'd want to…"

"I'd love to."

"I hoped you'd say that."

Standing next to a table in the library advising an inmate researching her legal options, I glanced down the aisle at a beautiful, busy Natifah. I knew she was a perfectionist, and she liked all the books in place, so I knew she'd catch the book in that aisle that was not. I had to bite the inside of my cheek to keep from smiling when she got to the book I purposely moved. She dropped her head and smiled bashfully when she saw the purple paper butterfly I'd placed in between the pages. I watched as she kissed it before turning slightly to slide it in her pocket. Just as I was about to make my way towards her to steal some smooches, Lewis' loud-mouth ass came through the door of the library, pulling a cart.

"Whaddup, bruh? You in here dying of boredom yet?" he asked, coming to a stop not far from him.

"Excuse me for a minute, Bates," I told the slightly older woman, whose dislike of Lewis showed on her face. "Not yet – with ya rude ass. I was helping her work on something."

"She is aiight. These hoes ain't got nothing but time," he cracked while looking in Bates' direction as he laughed.

"I swear you's an ignant negro. Just because they're behind bars doesn't mean they don't deserve respect." I returned, annoyed with his presence already.

"I don't respect any hoe that needs my permission to eat and shit. Shit, some of these bitches lucky I let them touch this slithering snake I'm packin'," he said and even grabbed his dick while looking in Bates' direction.

"Is there something you needed, or did you come down here just to prove how much of an asshole you can be?" I spat.

"Actually, I came to bring this delivery for your goody two shoes, last boy scout ass to handle. But trust, I ain't interested in staying." Lewis said as he nodded at the cart and took a step back to walk away. "Hold up! Damn…maybe I *will* stay. I see the library has a lil something sexy in here I wouldn't mind learning more about."

Following his line of sight, I saw Fatima standing on her toes trying to place books on the top shelf. Instantly, I saw red, and my blood began to boil.

"She fine as fuck – even for an inmate!" Lewis exclaimed. "Aye, let me get the key to the storeroom. I'mma get ol' girl to help me with getting this cart up in there. See what she hittin' for."

"Nah, we ain't doin' that up in here, and not on my watch. You can leave the cart here or take it and leave it by the door for me to handle," I instructed.

I had to bring it down a bit, not to cause any suspicion, but this nigga was asking for me to fuck him up. Not only did his ass not deserve to be in Natifah's space, but he also didn't deserve to even sniff the pussy. Besides, that shit was all mine, and I didn't share.

"Whatever, church boy." Lewis sputtered, looking me up and down. "Since that's the energy you comin' with, I'mma leave this right here for you," he added with a pat on my shoulder.

"Gee, thanks."

"All I know is ya ass is stupid. I'd be up in here wearin' that ass out. She is fine as frog hair – unlike some of these other tore up ass hoes. Ain't that right, Bates?" he asked and laughed. "See you on break bruh."

"Asshole," Bates said lowly as she shook her head.

"Usually, I might have a comment about you saying that, but I agree."

LATER IN THE DAY, when I thought I would have some time with Natifah, I had another visitor. When the warden walked in, I almost shit a brick – but I played it cool. I continued helping an inmate after greeting him before he disappeared down an aisle. He returned just a couple of minutes later and asked to see me in the hub. I excused myself from the inmate and followed him inside.

"How can I help you, sir?" I questioned, maintaining my cool.

"I wanted to speak with you about something that was brought to my attention," he began before there was a knock at the door.

"Yes, come in!" he yelled out.

"You… uh, wanted to see me, warden?" Natifah asked nervously.

"I did. It had been brought to my attention by several inmates… that they've never seen the library so organized and outdated. As a result of that, the library is being restocked with more materials for inmates to utilize. You were to be moved to kitchen detail next week, but I think your purpose is best served here in the library. So, good job," the warden offered her with a smile.

"Thank you, warden," she returned bashfully.

"The first shipment of new materials came today, with more to come in the next few days. Pratt, if you don't mind assisting Inmate Foxworth with some of the heavy lifting, I'd like for her to tackle the library renovation…of sorts."

"That's not a problem, sir," I replied – inwardly happy as hell. That meant more time alone with my boo.

"The old editions of the books can be stored in the storage room. I do realize it's quite a mess, so Foxworth – if you can take care of that as well, it'd be a great help. I did hear about your upcoming court date, so my character letter as a thank you for your hard work, will certainly go a long way," he informed her with a smile.

"Thank you so much, sir. That would be greatly appreciated."

"Thank you," he returned with a nod. "That'll be all," was added, excusing Natifah.

"Even in prison wear that's a looker there," the warden said, causing me to want to punch him in his shit too. "You know why I picked you for this project, right?"

"Because I'm dependable?" I guessed.

"That, and because Lewis is an asshole. I've been hearing talk about him amongst some of the inmates. If I come across any evidence that the rumors are true, I'm bouncin' his ass outta here before he can blink. You have integrity, Pratt. I appreciate that."

"Thank you so much, sir. I appreciate the compliment."

"Just keep up the good work. The next shipment will be in tomorrow, and it's a big one. So, you might want to have Foxworth start clearing space in the storeroom today."

"I'll be sure to pass on that assignment as soon as I'm done with my hourly report."

"Good man," he offered, patting my shoulder. "Carry on."

Oh, I'm gonna carry on like a muthafucka...all up in my boo's sweet pussy. I thought to myself as I stood to walk him to the door.

As soon as the warden left out the door of the library, the smile I was keeping at bay showed itself. I regained my composure before I turned around to walk back towards Natifah. I stopped at the table to check on Bates, then made my way to Natifah to deliver the warden's message. Luckily, she was working in my former nap corner, away from the cameras.

"Is everything okay?" she rushed out softly with a concerned look on her face.

"Everything's cool, ma. Especially since we'll be spending more time together. You heard the man. I need to help you with the heavy lifting." I said with a devilish grin on my face.

"Aaah. Well, you are very good at heavy lifting," she flirted back.

"The warden wants you to start organizing that other storeroom since we'll need the space. You let me know when you're ready to get started. I'll be over here working with Bates." I informed her before stealing a quick kiss.

"I can't wait until you're working me," she cooed before brushing her hand over my dick as she placed a book on the shelf.

"How you gonna send me over there with a hard dick?" I enquired while grinning. "Damn, you turn me on."

"Ditto, handsome."

"Let me hurry up and get her ass outta here. I got something I need to handle…asap."

When I approached inmate Bates to see if she needed my help any further, she told me she was wrapping it up for the day. I'd left the cart Lewis had brought in earlier nearby, so as she got up to replace her books on the shelf, I began pushing it towards the storeroom as Bates headed towards Natifah.

"Thank you so much for your suggestions. You're a blessing." I heard Bates say to Natifah.

"Anytime. I'm here if you need me, and I came across a couple other research books that may help you as well," was Natifah's sweet reply.

"Can I borrow you tomorrow for a little while?" Bates asked, a little too flirty for my liking.

"Ain't like I have anywhere else to be." Natifah cracked, and they shared a laugh.

"See you tomorrow." Bates offered as she walked off. "Thank you too, Officer Pratt. You need help with that?" she hollered down the hall as I pushed the heavy cart on wheels.

"I got this. You just make sure you stay outta trouble, so all this research isn't for nothing." I offered.

Bates was cool peeps; and from what she told me about her case, her attorney definitely dropped the ball.

"Roger that. See you tomorrow," she threw over her shoulder as she walked towards the library exit.

I HAD JUST GOTTEN the door open to the storage room and was muscling the cart through the door when I felt her presence behind me. She was pushing a smaller cart of her own, looking at me with a look of lust in her eyes. Once she got her cart through the door and let it close behind her, I was on her ass. With her pressed against the door, we kissed hungrily. She busied her hands with unbuckling my belt and unzipping my pants as my tongue danced with hers while I filled a hand with her perky breast.

When I felt her soft hands slowly stroking my dick, it immediately hardened from her touch. Untying her pants, I slid them over her ass and down her legs. As soon as her bottom was bare, I lifted her by her thighs and sat her right down on all this big dick.

"Oh… baby, you feel…so…good," she moaned as I thrust into her. Lifting her with each stroke.

"My God…this pussy…is…. Ooooou," I moaned out like a lil bitch when she tightened her walls around my member.

Moving from in front of the door, due to the racket my thrusts were making, she began doing more dick riding than I was thrusting. Her butter-soft hands touched my face as she looked lovingly into my eyes before her lips were on mine. She sucked on my tongue once I offered it to her and worked this dick like it had never been worked before.

"Ooooou shit, Daddy. I'm… I'm cumin," she keened softly.

"Cum all over daddy's dick. This *your* dick. Cream all on this mufucka." I lamented as I looked into her eyes as she struggled to keep them open. "This my pussy?" I asked as I stroked my way to my climax.

"Yes, daddy. Even outside of these walls…it's yours," she groaned in response.

That answer was more than enough to incite me to do exactly what I said I was gonna do earlier. I carried on in that tight, wet, warm, juicy wonder pussy. I carried on so much that I didn't care about the sound of skin slapping or her slightly heightened moans. And I didn't care that she'd cummed again, and so much that her juices were sliding down my thighs.

"Can I cum, baby?" I asked, feeling my nut rising from my toes.

"Yes, daddy. Give it to me," she stammered before she tightened her grip around my pole and began matching my thrust.

"Ahhhh fuck! Shhhhhhiiiiiiiiiiiiiit!" I hissed as I filled her with my seeds.

With my dick still inside her and her legs wrapped around me, I laid on her chest panting. Listening to her heartbeat as she gently rubbed her hand over my hair and held me with her other arm.

"Natifah…" I began.

"I do like you; and I think when you get out of here – if you're open it – we see where this can go," I revealed to her sincerely.

"I'm happy to hear that because I like you too. I'd love to see where life takes us and the sex we'll have in a bed," she replied with a smile.

"Shit. I'm damn near scared of what that pussy do now." I cracked, finally leaving her body and letting her down.

"I'm the one that should be scared…king ding-a-ling."

"I think I like the sound of that," I said with a hand on my beard and a raised eyebrow.

"I like the sound of you moaning for me," she cooed sexily. "That shit makes me so wet for you."

"Aiight now, don't get it up again. You know what has to go down."

"Well…" she began before dropping slowly to her knees. "Consider it up," she added before she began slowly sucking her juices from my member.

"Oh Lawd."

Chapter 5

hen I walked into the prison that Tuesday morning, my heart was inwardly smiling. I didn't get to see Natifah the day before because she had a court date, which I was anxious to hear about. I also had a little surprise set up for her. I knew I had it bad when I decided to put my job on the line to do something to make my lady feel special. Yeah, I said it…my lady. I'm claiming all that fine-ness.

I got to the library a few minutes before Natifah was scheduled to come in for work. After quickly throwing my things in the office, I went to the storeroom to make sure things were in order. I locked the door behind me and headed back to the hub to do my start-of-shift reports. When I emerged from between an aisle of books, she was walking through the door, looking beautiful as ever. The way her face lit up and she blushed when she saw me made me wanna take her ass right then on top of one of those tables – but I played it cool.

"Good morning, Officer Pratt. You look especially handsome today," she said softly.

"Good morning, beautiful. How are you today?" I asked with a slight smile.

"Even better since my favorite officer is here," she replied, still not coming any closer.

"So, you know I've been waiting to hear. How'd court go yesterday?"

"Wellllll…." she began before we were interrupted.

"Special delivery, nigga!" Lewis perked as he pulled a large cart filled with boxes behind him. "Is this what y'all corny asses waiting for?"

"I'll go work on the shelves until I need to start on the delivery," Natifah said faintly before dropping her head and walking away.

"Well damn. What, her ass got social anxiety or some shit?" Lewis asked, still watching her like a hawk. "She seems type of weird to me. She ever talk to you?"

"Besides to ask a question, and that's if she has to, she doesn't say much. She's good with the other inmates though." I replied before turning my attention to the cart so his ass couldn't see how pissed I was.

"I bet you I can get her ass to open right on up. Why don't

you go take a smoke break from being a boy scout or some shit? Let me holla at her for a minute. Feel me?" he checked, nudging me with his elbow.

"Nah…but what I'mma do for you is give you a warning. I ain't say shit, even though I'm a boy scout and all, but the warden done got wind of some of your bullshit. If I were you, I'd be more concerned with keeping your job than you are trying to crack for some ass." I seethed, trying to keep my cool.

"Get the fuck outta here!" Lewis said loudly and cracked up laughing until he saw my face. "You serious?"

"Yeah, I am – but you ain't get that shit from me. Just putting you up on game." I offered with a shrug before I started pulling the cart towards the back of the library.

I wasn't moving fast enough though. That cart was heavy than a muthafucka. I guess my anger was propelling me to move it as much as I did.

"Yo, what else he say? You sure you ain't say shit?" he asked, now all panicked.

"Nah, I ain't say shit, and *you* better not say shit. It's just hearsay at this point, but he said if he gets evidence, your ass is black history." I warned, trying to keep from laughing.

His cocky, ignant, loudmouth, pervert ass walked around this prison like he owned the joint. So to see his ass standing there looking around with his eyes bulging out of his head, looking like Smokey in Deebo's pigeon coop, was a sight to see.

"Fuck, man! Yo, good lookin' out, Pratt. Will you uh…let me know if you hear anything else? My mouth is shut," he damn near begged.

"I got you, bruh. Just chill the fuck out." I warned.

"Word," he agreed. "Let me get outta here so I can go be on my boy scout shit too. I need these coins my nigga, and I ain't prison material. Real talk."

"Aiight. I'll holla."

With the library being empty, and it was getting close to lunch, I approached Natifah as she worked in the back row of the library, near the storeroom. I just stood and admired her for a moment as she worked with her back towards me.

"So, are you gonna stand there and stare or are you gonna speak?" she asked, obviously feeling my presence.

"I was admiring the view for a second, before I invited you to lunch," I replied with a smile.

"Invite me to lunch? As much as I'd love that, how is that even possible?"

"You let big daddy worry about that. Just skip mess hall. I got you, bae." I said proudly with a grin.

"When you put it like that, I'll be there," was her toothy reply before she began blushing.

"See you in a bit."

～

I FELT like a school kid waiting for the final bell to ring as lunch approached. As soon as noon hit, I headed to the entrance of the library and locked up for the next hour. I damn near speed walked down the aisles until I found Natifah, who smiled when I appeared before her.

"Hey, handsome," she said and offered a smile.

"Hey, beautiful. You ready for lunch?"

"I am. Lead the way, big daddy," she cooed.

"Mmmmm. You make sure you keep that same energy in just a little bit." I cracked as I unlocked the storage room door.

Bypassing the main storage room, I unlocked the extra space room that the warden had us clear out. I had smuggled a couple of blankets from the laundry area and made a pallet on the floor. I couldn't bring in a picnic basket, so an insulated lunch cooler had to do. I did the best I could, given the circumstances to make it romantic, and I must've done a good job because when I looked at Natifah, she had tears in her eyes.

"Baby. This is beautiful and probably the sweetest thing anyone has ever done for me. Thank you," she beamed before kissing me.

"It's my pleasure. I wish I could've done more."

"This is perfect, big daddy," she teased.

I sat down on the blanket first, then reached out my hand to help her sit. It wasn't a five-star restaurant lunch, but the hoagies I got from a popular Italian spot near me, sour cream and onion chips – which she mentioned were her favorite –

and peach lemonade were far better than what they serve up in the mess hall. It was refreshing to see a woman so appreciative of the little things.

"Oh…how'd court go?" I asked as I watched her enjoy her lunch. "We were interrupted when you were about to tell me earlier."

"Oh…it's nothing. Except the judge granted my appeal and I have a new trial coming up," she beamed. "My lawyer thinks that I have a good chance of getting outta here."

"That's the best news I've heard all day." I beamed, genuinely happy for her. "So, any news on your court date?"

"Thirty days," was her response along with a sigh. "It's gonna be the longest thirty days of my life. Well, second. The first thirty in here felt like an eternity."

"I can't even imagine. The good thing is all of this will be behind you very soon. All you'll have to worry about is the bright, successful future ahead." I said and raised my lemonade to toast her.

"Thank you, babe. I'm trying not to get too excited…just in case. I don't want to get my hopes up for nothing."

"It's not for nothing. Shit, you even winning your appeal is a damn good sign. You're outta here! I just hope that when you are, we… Well…" I began until she placed a finger over my lips.

"I meant every word I said, and I can't wait to be with you outside of these walls."

"Well, we've got enough time for me to give you just a

taste of what you'll receive. Now… Lunchtime is over. Strip." I ordered sexily.

"You heard me. Strip." I repeated as I stood to do the same.

"Mmmmmm…" she moaned, watching me as I shed my clothing. Once I was naked, I laid down on the floor and told her, "Sit on big daddy's face."

"As you wish…big daddy."

I watched, damn near salivating at the mouth as she straddled my chest, with her back facing me. Backing up until she felt my hands on her hips, she allowed me to lower her sweet pussy onto my face. Darting my tongue into her opening first, I then attached myself to her clit. Using my tongue to apply pressure at first, I began to lap at her swollen nub as she began to moan. At first, when she moved, I thought she was trying to escape this hurricane tongue, but boy was I mistaken. As she leaned forward, I was allowed even more open access to her sweet pussy but feeling her warm mouth working its way down my throbbing, hard dick made it hard to concentrate. The sound of subtle moans and the slurping sounds she made as she devoured my dick filled the storeroom. After a powerful orgasm shook her body, and she rewarded me with a job well done by cumming all in my mouth, I pushed her down to my dick, which was standing at attention.

Instead of riding all this dick with her back towards me, she swiveled around until she faced me. I licked her juices off my lips as I watched her align the swollen head of my dick with her opening before lowering herself onto it. I was hypnotized as I watched her hula hoop on my dick with her eyes closed as she bit her bottom lip. Placing my hand on her stomach, I used my thumb to play with her clit as she moved against it.

"Oh… God… I love you, big daddy," she moaned.

Yes! I cheered in my head because I thought I was the only one feeling that way. Knowing she felt the same only made my dick harder.

"I love you too, ma. I do…and I love the way… Damn you working this dick." I commended, losing my train of thought.

Sitting up, I gently grabbed a hand full of her curly hair, leaning her neck back as I kissed and sucked on her neck before moving to her nipples. My toes continued to twitch as it felt like her pussy gripped me tighter with every movement. I had to kiss her lips to keep from screaming out like a bitch the way she had me feeling. Then it was my turn. I flipped her onto her back and began delivering power strokes. Using her hand, she covered her mouth to keep from screaming too loudly as she came again. The sound of me stirring her juices, as well as them painting my stomach, had my dick on super hard, and I couldn't get enough of her. Reluctantly leaving her body, I ordered her to, "Turn over." She moved to her knees, looking like a sexy ass panther, then lowered her chest to the floor, allowing me to see that beautiful ass spread.

"Damn… that's a thing of beauty." I groaned as she gave her ass a little wiggle.

Spanking a cheek lightly, I filled her to the hilt with a low grunt. The way her walls choked my dick had me questioning, "What the fuck?!" as I struggled not to cum.

"Oooo….big… big daddy. I'm cummin'…again," she cried.

I looked down to see my dick disappear inside of her glistening, pink opening and reappear covered in her sweet, creamy goodness.

"Look how my pussy shows out for daddy. This big daddy's pussy, ma?" I asked as I kept stroking, feeling my nut rise.

"Yes, big daddy. Yes!" she whisper-screamed as she came yet again. "Oooou… yes daddy. It's all yours."

"And this is your dick. All yours, ma." I returned as I realized there was no holding back the nut that was forthcoming. "Can I cum, ma?"

"Yes, baby. Cum for me."

"Ooooooou shit. Oooooooooou!" I groaned as I came so hard, feeling like it came from the base of my spine. "Damn, this pussy is my kryptonite," I added as I left her body and had to sip my drink. A brother was parched.

"I don't know what this dick is, but I'm happy it's mine," was Natifah's reply as she lay on her side, looking at me lovingly.

"Jabril, I know I said…."

"I meant it… but if you…"

"It's my turn to interrupt. Although it was said in a

moment of absolute passion, I meant what I said too. I love you, Officer Pratt."

"I love you too, Natifah. None of that Officer Pratt shit unless it's necessary. I can't have my boo addressing me like that."

"I'm your boo now?" she asked with a smile as she got up to begin cleaning up and getting dressed, knowing our time was running short.

"I wanted to call you *my woman*, but I didn't ask, and I don't want to scare you away," I admitted.

"Well…." she began before she walked up to me and draped her arms around my shoulders before kissing me. "Why don't you ask and see what my answer is? It might surprise you."

"Okay. Natifah, will you be my woman? See just how far we can take this thang here we done started?"

"I don't know. This is all so sudden," she cracked and laughed. "Of course I will, babe."

"Then that's what it is. Hell yeah!" I beamed. "Oh…do me a favor and keep away from Lewis. He's already made a couple of remarks that almost had me want to break his jaw. The nigga has his eye on you."

"Oh, I've heard a few inmates talking about him. I already planned to stay as far away from him as possible. No worries there. Besides, I already have the man I want," she cooed and kissed my lips again.

"Damn, I love them kisses. Give me another one." I

requested, with my dick on hard again already as I filled both hands with her soft cheeks.

"Oh no you don't. Lunch is almost over. We need to start making it look like we've been doing some work instead of puttin' *in* work." She said as she playfully pushed me away.

"I like the way you put that." I beamed. "Big daddy be puttin' in work, huh?"

"Mmmmm, does he," she licked her lips. "But Daddy has to keep it in his pants for now. Maybe before the days end, we can…."

"Hell yeah. I'm kickin' everybody outta this bitch early."

"You're a mess," was her response, along with a laugh. "I love my mess though."

"Your mess loves you too. Now, back to work… Unless you wanna…"

"See ya later, babe."

"Oooou shit! Daddy…. Ooooou…. have mercy!" Natifah cried out as she tried to pry my face away from her pussy.

"Unh uh!" I mumbled from between her thick lips as I slapped the side of her ass to scold her.

I had Natifah's sexy ass atop a pile of books, and my arm wrapped around her thighs to keep her from trying to escape this tongue lashing she was receiving. I was obsessed with eating her pussy. The way she came and how frequently she came was an aphrodisiac in itself. I'd never had a woman respond to me the way she did. Once her legs began shaking and her back began to arch, I knew she was about to bust her biggest nut. When she began grinding subtly against my tongue, I knew she was about to blow.

"Gotdamn!" I growled out as her pussy squirted for big daddy for the first time and she fell limp. "Hell yeah! Look at what big daddy done did." I added, proud of my handy worth.

"See, now I'm too tired for dick," she said between pants.

"Say what?" I perked.

"The devil is a lie. Lay that big ol' pipe on Mama."

"That shit turns me the fuck on when you take charge." I gritted as I stood there with my dick feeling like it was ready to bust out my pants on its own.

"Oh yeah? Sit down in that chair so mama can get him nice and wet with this mouth before I climb on," she sexily ordered.

"Yes ma'am."

Doing as I was told, I sat in the chair and watched my beauty drop to her knees in front of me. After freeing my dick, she reached up for my face to kiss me deeply, on some sweet shit. Seconds later that shit went out of the window, and she turned into a certified head monster.

"What the...fuck..." I moaned as she used her tongue to do some shit that had my toes tingling.

"Mmmmm..." she hummed when she felt my dick pulse in her mouth.

I held on to the chair because there was nothing else I could do to escape her mouth, and you know a brother couldn't go out like that.

"Bring big daddy his pussy. I need to feel you, **now**." I demanded, breathily.

"Yes sir," she complied as she straddled my lap.

Grabbing her ass cheeks, I slammed her right down on my dick, causing her to gasp. We fucked and kissed each other on some sexy-ass aggressive shit. As Natifah was about to cum, I watched in awe as she palmed her breasts and bit her bottom lip. I could fuck her forever just off that vision alone, but the nut that she was working out of me, had other plans.

"Aww fuck, ma. Fuuuuuck!" I groaned as she bounced on my dick until I grabbed her hips one last time before filling her with my seeds. "Damn girl."

"What did I do?" she asked with a smile before she began kissing my neck and then my lips.

"Baby…lunch is…almost over, and you getting him hard again," I replied reluctantly, already growing inside of her.

"You're right. I should stop," she said and quickly hopped off my lap.

That shit left me dumbfounded. Yeah, I had opened my mouth, but now my dick was hard again, and I was feeling a way. So, when she bent over to grab her pants from the floor, I slid this big dick up in her and served her up some long strokes.

"Oooou…. yes big….daddy," she stuttered as she threw it back. Her ass knew what she was doing, knowing that a nigga was gonna cum quick.

"Fuck! Throw that shit, ma," I encouraged, unable to resist spankin' that ass as it waved at me with each stroke. "I'm bout to cum, bae. Shiiiiiiit!" I hissed, as I thrust so hard into her, she now stood on her toes.

"Let's cum.... together, daddy. I'm.... cummin'..." she moaned, as I felt my juices rush from my body and mix with hers.

"Oou you nasty." I teased.

"You like it."

"Nah, I *love* that shit," I said and kissed her lips before I quickly wiped off and got dressed. "I'll see you out there. I've gotta open the door."

"Just take a second helping of goodies and run, huh?" she cracked.

"Never that – but you started it."

JUST AS THE LIBRARY EMPTIED, and I was planning on getting another fix to last me through the night, I saw the warden on camera coming through the door. I was happy as hell that he came during the time I did my end-of-shift reports, and we were working instead of fucking.

"Officer Pratt. How are things this afternoon?" the warden asked.

"Pretty good, sir. Nice and quiet."

"As a library should be," he returned with a nod. "I know it's only been a couple of weeks, and there's a lot of ground to cover, but I stopped by to see how our library revamp is going.

We have some state folks wanna come by and make sure the donations are being allocated correctly," he informed me as he made air quotes.

"I can finish up my report and take you around." I offered.

"That'd be great. I won't take up too much of your time."

"It's not a problem," I said as I stood to take him around.

I took him around to each section of the library where he could see that half the shelves were empty, and the other half filled with the newer books. Natifah had even made signs to alphabetize each aisle and even separated law books from others. I purposely saved the storeroom for last, hoping Natifah saw us combing the aisles and went in there to make sure there was no evidence of our daily fuck fests. When we arrived at the already propped open storage room door, Natifah was sliding a metal shelf in place against a back wall to begin filling with the older books that were to be stored in the room.

"Are you sure you should be moving that alone?" the warden asked in a worried tone, not wanting her to be injured.

He was barely hanging onto his job, and reports of cruelty, unsafe work environment, or any other that shit weren't something he could afford to deal with. Of course, we ain't supposed to know nothing about that.

"It's not that heavy at all, and it slides pretty easy across the concrete floor." Natifah answered, softly.

"I've gotta say, I'm impressed. You've gotten more done

than I expected. Do you think by next week the library will be ready for state visitors?" he asked.

"I'll see to it that it is. And thank you so much for your letter, warden. I really appreciate it," she said and reached out her hand to shake his.

"With what you've gotten done here – and saving my neck a little bit – you've got another one coming. So, thank you. I guess it's a good thing we're getting this done now. You may be outta here soon. This place will miss you."

"Thank you, sir."

"You're quite welcome," he returned with a nod. "I'll leave you to it. Pratt, be a good man and walk an old guy out."

"Sure thing, sir."

I quickly puckered my lips at Natifah before disappearing out the door behind the warden. Strolling through the aisles, he again complimented me on being one of his good employees, before adding, "Which is why I shouldn't ask this."

"I'm sorry, sir?"

"That girl has singlehandedly transformed this place, and I want to reward her for her work. It ain't much, but maybe you might be able to order yourself some lunch and get something extra you'd share with her. Give her a break from prison food for a day. Am I overstepping asking this of you?"

"Not at all, sir. She is a hard worker… and stubborn."

"Aren't all these new age women?" he returned as he shook his head. "Bring me the receipt for it and I'll cover it – for your hassle."

"Thank you, sir."

"Thank you. There's one last shipment Lewis should be on his way down here with shortly. To make sure we stay on schedule for our special guests, I'd like to close the library early tomorrow if we could and make sure our girl keeps up the good work."

"Will do."

"Okay. Carry on," he said with a wave as he left out of the door.

That nigga just didn't know how I be carrying on up in that storeroom. Shit, as soon as I was finished with these reports, I'm gonna cut up some more before the day was done. Not to mention, his ass just made it more than easy for me to have my way with my woman tomorrow without the possibility of any interruptions. I swear I wanted to hug that man – but nah. All my lovin' was for the bronze beauty with the booty back there stacking books, who I was just about to make my way to when the library door was pulled open with force.

"Yo. Was that the warden I just saw leaving here?" Lewis asked nervously as he struggled with yet another oversized cart of boxes.

"Yeah, it was."

"He say anything else about me? Fill a nigga in," he rushed out.

"You need to chill out."

"That's easy for you to say. Your head ain't on the chopping block," he spat as he pulled the cart by me.

Little did he know, I was right next to him on the chopping block – only my shit hadn't been discovered, and I'm in love with my woman. He ain't need to know all that though.

"I feel you, but you look crazy paranoid bruh. He only mentioned some state people were coming by next week to make sure the library funds and supplies were used correctly. Oh, and that you were on your way with another delivery." I replied.

I know I wasn't shit for it, but I was enjoying watching Lewis wiggle on the hook. He talked to and treated the inmates like shit. Not to mention the ones he took advantage of. Inmates or not, everyone deserves respect. He gave none, and only got it from those that feared him. Oh, and he kept lusting after my woman. Since I couldn't whip his ass for doing that, under the circumstances, his paranoia was the best punishment for now.

"Cool…cool. Good lookin' out. Let me know if you hear anything else," he pleaded as he came to a stop with the cart.

"You got it." I returned with a nod.

"My man," he said with a smile and extended a fist for me to bump. "I'mma holla at ya later."

"Yup," I mumbled.

I'd already peeped what aisle Natifah was working in, so when I noticed him staring back as he walked out, I already knew what he was looking at. At least his ignant ass was trying to keep his bullshit undercover, but I peeped that shit. He knew I peeped it too because when he looked back at me and smirked, my eyes were locked dead on his ass. I made a mental note to make sure shit was secure when Natifah and I were getting it in. A desperate man was a dangerous man. So, if he got any inkling there was even a possibility anything was going on between me and Natifah, he would serve my ass up to save him with the quickness.

I finished the reports I started before the warden came in, allowing enough time for Lewis' sneaky ass to be gone before I left the hub. I grabbed the last cart and started towards the storeroom. I thought Natifah was in an aisle working, but she was already in the storeroom. When I walked in, she looked in my direction and gave me this sexy ass look that immediately made my dick jump. She didn't say a word, she just kept working and looking at me periodically as she bit her bottom lip sexily. When she leaned forward to gather her long, curly tresses into a messy bun, I couldn't take it anymore. I walked up to her like she was a nigga on the street that owed me money and pulled her into the extra storage space. I closed the door behind us, gently pushed her against the wall, and kissed her hungrily as I freed my dick. Turning her around, I pulled her pants down and backed her towards me before placing my hand on her back to bend her over. There was no foreplay, but I'd come to know my pussy, and I knew it was already wet for big daddy.

Unable to wait any longer to be inside of her, I filled her with one thrust, lifting her from her feet. Tilting her pelvis as she held onto to the wall, I began stroking her slow and deep.

My dick glistened with her juices as I watched it move in and out of her tight hole.

"Do you see…what the fuck…you do to…me, ma?" I asked as I stroked with precision.

"Yes Daddy," she moaned out, sexy as hell. "You do…the same. Oh God… I love…the way…you're fuckin'…me…" she struggled to get out.

"Damn, I wanna crawl up and live in this…juicy…mutha-fucka." I moaned, already feeling myself about to cum. "This is gonna be a quick one, ma. I ain't lock…the door. Ooou… fuck." I gritted.

"I'm already… Big daddy, I'm cummin'," she moaned softly before coating my dick with her creamy goodness.

"That's what big daddy likes to…see. Ahhhhhhhh!" I gritted as my seeds rushed from my body and into hers as my toes twitched in my work boots. "I'm sorry it had to be a quickie, ma. I'mma give it to you real good tomorrow. I got something in store for that ass." I added as I pulled her close for a kiss.

"You always give it to me good," she cooed as she looked into my eyes while stroking my beard before she kissed me.

"You love me?" I asked, already knowing the answer.

"I do love you."

"I love you more, ma." I returned and kissed her again. "I'mma help you with some of this shit. The warden is trippin' because some state folks coming in here next week. He wants to make sure it's done. So, the library is only open for the first half of the day tomorrow. The second half, that ass belongs to me. We gonna do some work and put *in* work."

"Mmmm. Say that shit Daddy," she moaned, making my dick jerk again.

"Cut that sexy shit out and get back to work. I'll be back to steal my goodnight kiss before shift is over."

"You better."

WHEN I TELL you the struggle was real trying to focus on the doing work part of the day, shit was real. It had been a few weeks since Natifah and I started this thing of ours, and I swear a nigga was hooked. When I was here at work, all I wanna do was be up under her. When I was home, all I thought about was being inside of her. Now that she was within my reach, and I couldn't touch her – thanks to a few inmates being in the library – was torture. I couldn't wait to clear house and get to the puttin' in work part of the day; and thankfully, there was only one hour until lunchtime.

I left her in the storeroom and headed out to check in on the inmates and to order lunch. I knew the warden was gonna raise an eyebrow if I ordered too extravagant of a lunch, so I placed a bullshit order for a couple of hot sandwiches, chips, and sodas before placing a separate order. I gave specific instructions for the order to come in the same bag with two separate receipts. The cheapest of the two would go to the warden. When I finished that, with a smile on my face, I went out to instruct the inmates to finish up what they were working on because we were closing soon to prepare for a state visit. They glanced around and saw the boxes of boxes throughout the library as if they thought I was lying.

"How come I can't come work in here? I can be helpful and spend some time with you," an inmate named Africa said before looking me up and down, licking her lips.

"You know you outta pocket." I scolded. "I could write you up for that, but I won't be petty. In case you didn't already know the rules, fraternizing with inmates is a criminal offense."

"Well damn. I guess someone needs to tell some of the other COs in here that." Africa spat with a roll of her eyes.

Hell, I should be rolling my eyes at her offering that rancid, ran-through snatch she walking around here giving out like its bubble gum. She did not discriminate, so she was fucking other inmates, and COs from what I heard.

"Come on, girl. His boy already said he was a goody two shoes, so you wasting your time. Making me sit up in here all this time and you ain't getting no play," the inmate sitting at the table with her griped. "Bring your ass. Maybe we can still get some time in the yard."

"Have a good day, ladies." I offered as they got up from the table, leaving the books they were so-called reading behind.

Just as the door closed behind the dirty birds, the phone in the hub rang. I rushed in to pick it up, and it was the desk calling to let me know our lunch had arrived. Natifah was in the storeroom working her ass off, so I didn't bother to go back to let her know I was stepping out. I knew I could trust her, so I headed out the door to pick up our order. I also was in such a rush to get back and climb up in my pussy that I didn't lock the door behind myself, but I'd only be gone five minutes anyway – or so I thought. I seemed to run into every co-worker who wanted to have a conversation on my way to the desk. The shit was annoying as hell, but I couldn't be rude.

When I did get to the desk, I grabbed the bag, said a quick hello to the desk sergeant, and made my way back to the library. I grabbed the sign I made to put on the door, letting everyone know the library was closed, and made my way back to the storeroom. When I got back there, I saw *red*.

"Bitch, you making this harder than it needs to be." Lewis seethed as he held a crying Natifah against the wall as he fumbled with his pants.

"Muthafucka, you better step the fuck away from her *right now* or I'll **kill** you where you stand." I seethed, having dropped the bag, and balled up my fist.

"You ain't killin' shit, nigga, and this ain't what it looks like. This a lil game we like to play when your last boy scout ass ain't around," this lyin' ass nigga said as he fixed his pants. "Ain't that right, boo?" he asked Natifah as he reached out to touch her, causing her to flinch. **"Answer me, bitch!"** he roared.

I was trying to keep the hellfire that was raging inside me from beating his ass on sight and keeping my job; but what kind of man would I be to let this shit go unpunished? So, I did what any man who loved his woman would do if she was hurt.

"Natifah," I called her name calmly, but she just stood there, staring blankly. "Natifah!"

"Yes?" she said in an almost childlike voice.

"I need you to go into the hub, pick up the black phone, and dial 9. Tell them Officer Pratt asked you to call in for an assist, immediately. Go unlock the library door then go sit at the front desk with your hands on the table and do not move. Do you understand me?" I asked sternly.

"Yes."

"Good. Go now." I commanded.

I watched her scale the wall so she would not get anywhere near Lewis before she took off crying out of the storeroom. As soon as she was outta sight, I walked up to Lewis and tore into his ass.

"She ain't nothin' but a prison bitch, nigga! Fuck her!" Lewis yelled as he tried to block my blows.

"Nah…fuck you. Pervert, rapist ass nigga!" I barked before I hit his ass with a Mike Tyson-type uppercut, laying that nigga out.

"Come on, man! Over a bitch?!" he yelled out of his bleeding mouth. "Come on, Pratt…we supposed to be cool. Tell 'em she was tryin' to give me the pussy when you came in. It's our word against hers! Do you know what the fuck they can do to me?!"

"You should've thought about that before you came in here trying to take pussy…bitch ass nigga!"

"I'm a bitch ass nigga, but you a pussy!" he barked before spitting blood on my boot.

That disrespectful shit brought him a two-piece and another trip to the floor. I stood over him breathing fire, wanting to stomp the shit outta his dumb ass as he lay on the floor still coppin' pleas. Those shits damn sure fell on death ears. He could tell that shit to the judge.

"What in the holy fuck is going on in here?!" the warden yelled.

"Sir, I returned from the desk after grabbing my lunch order and interrupted Officer Lewis here in the process of attempting to rape Inmate Natifah Foxworth," I replied, stern as hell, still wanting to fuck Lewis' pervert ass up some more.

"You've gotta be fuckin' kiddin' me! With the state coming in here next week?! Get this piece of shit up and in a holding cell until I contact the state police," the warden ordered the guards that accompanied him.

"A holding cell?! Man…this nigga lyin'! And that bitch lyin' too!" Lewis shouted as he resisted being cuffed.

"The only person I hear lyin' is your ass! I took one look at that woman and already knew what happened! She's out there fucked up!" the warden roared. "Get his bitch ass outta here."

"Sir, I accept responsibility for my putting my hand on Lewis. I came in and…"

"I would've done the same thing," the warden said as he placed a hand on my shoulder. "I'll need to speak with you and Inmate Foxworth to file an incident report. We'll get to it tomorrow, so she can… Can I even say calm down? Fuck! I can't believe this shit!" he snapped.

"Whatever you need, sir."

"Right now, I need to see if Foxworth needs medical attention. I'll speak with you again in a few minutes. Meanwhile, get someone from maintenance to come clean up this blood. I see the pervert's a bleeder."

I sat at the table writing out my statement, stealing glances at Natifah as she talked with the warden as she shed tears. All I wanted to do was run over to her and hold her. It crushed my soul to see her shaking the way that she was. Especially as I listened as she told the warden the details of her attack. When I finished my statement, I went into the hub to work on the hourly reports that weren't done, with all the commotion going on. As I walked by, we made eye contact, and I hoped my eyes conveyed all the things my mouth couldn't at the moment. As much as I wanted to be inside her, I just wanted to hold her even more.

Unfortunately, I didn't get the opportunity to.

lmost two weeks had passed since the incident – and when I tell you a brother was in a funk, I had it bad. Not only was I not able to hold or comfort the woman I loved, who needed me, but I hadn't seen her. Touched her. Felt her. Smelled her. Although the warden felt my actions were justified, I was suspended for the "obsessive force" I used against Lewis. I guess the warden's way of feeling better about following through with that bullshit decision was to pay me for the time off. Either way, I was happy to get back to work. To get back to Natifah. Of course, I found it ironic that my return was the day before the rescheduled state visit.

When I walked into the library, the first thing I did was look around, hoping she may have already been there waiting for me. But I had to shake my head at myself. How the hell would she get in without me opening it first? Chuckling at myself, I walked into the hub, stepping on a piece of paper. Lifting my foot, I saw it was a Post-it with a butterfly drawn on it. I again had to shake my head at myself, acting like a schoolboy with his first crush. But fuck that, Natifah did that to me, and I loved it. I stuck the note in my front pocket and began to log onto the computers for the day when I heard the heavy metal door of the library closing.

"Ah! Good man. Welcome back," the warden exclaimed. "Good morning."

"Good morning. It's good to be back," was my reply, even though I wanted to slap his old ass.

"It was an unfortunate incident, and my hands were tied as far as your discipline. I hope you understand and that you accept my compensation as a form of apologies…of sort," he offered, getting all flushed in the cheeks.

"Accepted, sir. Thank you. I appreciate you."

"And I appreciate all of your hard work – which is the reason for my visit. As you know, things were…a little out of sorts with everything that transpired – which luckily coincided with the death of one of the board's family members – so we had some more time," he began.

Ain't this some shit. I thought to myself as I swallowed the urge to punch him in his shit for saying some heartless bullshit like that – and prolonging telling me what's up with my woman.

"Sir, if I may ask. Is Inmate Foxworth okay?" I asked, hating to now refer to her as that.

"That's a resilient young woman, and yes, she's fine. Smart as a whip too. I looked into her case as well as her history, and it seems to me she never should've seen the inside of these walls. Sad business really," he replied with a shake of his head as if it bothered him. "Anyway, she'll be arriving shortly. She's already done a wonderful job of what she could by herself. Unfortunately, besides female officers, I get a lot of shit from other guards about details in here. So, the library will be closed today for the completion of the renovation. If you could again handle the heavy lifting so we can have this done, you'd be a lifesaver. If you need to work overtime, I'll allow it – although according to the budget we can't afford it. If you get my meaning," he finished with a wink.

"I don't think that will be a problem, sir. I don't mind helping out. Especially since you were so kind to accommodate me in my absence." I said and added the fakest smile I could muster.

"Just like I knew. You're a good man," the warden beamed before patting my shoulder. "Oh, if you head to the desk about noon, there'll be a lunch delivery. And if you could please give me a ring directly before the day's end, I'd appreciate it."

Knock! Knock!

As soon as I heard the first knock I looked up and right into her eyes. Her face flushed and she dropped her head to hide her smile, after seeing the warden was in our midst.

"Ah…there she is," the warden's dick ridin' ass perked. "Good morning to you. I hope you're well-rested and ready for work, Foxworth."

"I am, sir. I was just stopping in to say thank you and good morning to Officer Pratt before I headed back to the storeroom. I won't interrupt, sir," she said and stood straight.

"Please…relax a bit. It's not the Armed Forces. No worries, we're about done here. Unless there's something else you need before I go, Pratt."

"I think that about covers it, sir."

"Jolly good. I'll leave you two to finish strong," he offered with a final pat on the shoulder before turning to leave the hub. "Oh…Pratt."

"Yes sir?"

"Be sure to keep the door locked at all times. We don't need any other…mishaps happening. Wouldn't you say?"

"You're right, sir. Let me see you to the door and lock up behind you."

"Like I said…good man."

After listening to the warden spew a few more lines of his borderline inappropriate bullshit, I wished him a good day before grabbing the sign I'd previously made and placing it in the door's window. As soon as the lock turned, I made a b-line back into the library. For appearances on camera, I went up and down the aisles of the library to do a check. While doing that, I was impressed with all Natifah had done in the time I was gone. That girl was the truth. It appeared all of the aisles were re-labeled and organized, except the last two. When I walked into the storeroom, she'd done the damn thing in there too.

"Get your fine ass over here right now, woman," I said hungrily as soon as I walked in and stepped to the side.

"Yes sir." Was her eager reply before making her way over to me.

She draped her arms around my shoulders, and her fingers grazed the back of my neck, sending a chill down my spine. I looked into her eyes for a few moments before kissing her as if she would break.

"I love you so much, and I'm sorry I couldn't be here to comfort you. I'm sorry I couldn't do more." I said sincerely.

"Baby…you did all you could do under the circumstances. I know what you have at stake, so I couldn't hold that against you. Besides, you did break your foot all up in a pervert nigga's ass and get suspended over me," she joked and chuckled lightly.

"I'd do it again in a heartbeat. When I came in here and…" I began but had to stop. "What's most important is that you're okay, and I'm here with you in this moment. I love you, Natifah."

"I love you more, Jabril," was her reply before she put those sexy ass lips on mine and kissed me deeply. "So…your pussy has been missing you and is feeling a type of way. Do we have to do work first before we put in work, or can Mama get an appetizer?"

"Climb on, beautiful. Big daddy got all the meat for you," was my reply with no hesitation, already having a hard dick as soon as the words left her mouth.

She kissed my lips hungrily, freeing my dick from my pants as I backed her into the smaller storage room. Kicking the door closed behind me, I backed her into the wall before slightly lifting her and bringing her to a landing on my ten inches. I watched the ecstasy on her face as she closed her eyes and bit her bottom lip as I thrust deep into her. God, that shit drove me crazy. Looking down into my eyes, her hands gently moved through my beard before she offered me her tongue as she began to match my stroke.

"Mmmm…my pussy so…fuckin' good," I mumble moaned between kisses.

"I missed you….and my dick, big daddy," she confessed as she began to work those hips.

"Ooooou shit. Ooooou." I moaned, feeling my toes tingle. "You tryna do me…dirty, huh? Aiight." I asked, bout ready to fuck some shit up.

"Unh huh," was her response.

Applying just the right amount of pressure between her, myself, and the wall, I began to power thrust in my pussy. I was balls deep and had her clawing at my back. Biting her lip wasn't gonna help with controlling her volume with the power of her impending orgasm, so she bit into my neck. That shit hurt and caught me off guard for a second, but that shit turned me the fuck on. What turned me on, even more, was the trail of fluids leaving her body and traveling down my leg before I felt her body relax, which was my cue to cum.

"Who's doin' who dirty now?" I boasted as I stroked her pulsing pussy until I felt my seeds rush from my body and enter hers.

"Mmm…" she purred before kissing me. "We needed that."

"Hell yeah, we did." I agreed before letting her down and handing her my handkerchief. "I guess I better get you some more wipes." I cracked.

"Not too many. Won't need them for much longer," she said with her back towards me.

"Come again?" I asked, having to stop fixing my shit to get clarification.

"Well…while you were gone, there's been some news regarding my case. Some great news actually," she beamed.

"Aiight woman, spill. You killin' me with the suspense right now." I damn near pleaded.

"I met with my attorney, who informed me that if everything goes according to plan, my case will be dismissed, and I'll be a free woman by the end of next week," she finally spit out.

"Are you fucking serious right now?!" I boomed, not giving a shit about my volume.

"As a heart attack. Mama's goin' home."

"It's finally happening. I'm so happy for you!" I

exclaimed, picking her up and twirling her around before kissing her.

"Thank you, baby. I'm pretty happy about it myself. I mean…I can't get fully happy until I officially hear those words, but I'm excited."

"So…where does that leave us?" I inquired, needing to know if we were still on the same page.

"What do you mean, *where does that leave us?* You think I go around giving out 'I love yous' and coochie-like its bubble gum?" she asked with a chuckle before shaking her head at me.

"I'm not saying it like that, babe. We talked about us being together even outside these walls. I want that more than anything. I'm just making sure you ain't got me handing out 'I love yous' and all this good dick, then you kick me to the curb." I half-cracked.

"Never that. You're my man, and I love you," she began as she gently touched my face. "Being with you, outside of this library, is what I dream about every night. You, and our love, have been my strength. There's no way I ever wanna lose that…or you."

"Damn, ma. If I wasn't already in love and pussy whipped, that statement right there would've done it. Fosho." I cracked and laughed, pulling her towards me. "I feel the same. You're my beautiful, black unicorn, and I ain't letting you go."

"Unh uh. See you playin'," she sassed. "I'm more of a mocha."

I couldn't help but crack up laughing at her silly ass. That was one of the things that made me love this woman. Even with being unjustly imprisoned, she had this coolness. This sense of humor. This vibe that made not loving her impossible.

"I swear I love your crazy ass," I said as I continued laughing.

"You better… and I love you too."

"Since you insisted on an appetizer, let's get to the do-work portion of the day so by the late afternoon, I can take my slow sweet time with my dessert." I teased.

"Mmmm damn. Say that shit, big daddy."

JUST SEEING Natifah again got me out of the funk I was in from not seeing her, but spending the whole day with just her and me – shooting the shit while working – gave me a glimpse of what I had to look forward to once we were together on the outside. Every time I looked in her direction, I envisioned her riding all this dick. Her D-cup breasts were still perky – and looking full as hell by the way – begging for me to suck on them. Because I didn't know what hating ass nigga – or otherwise – was watching for any little thing to fuck me over, I had to keep my lustful stares to a minimum. Something hard as hell.

So, when lunchtime came around, I was more than ready. Lucky for her I loved her, we had been working our asses off, and I knew she had to be hungry. If that hadn't been the case, she'd have to feed Big Daddy first… If you catch my drift.

"I'm gonna head down to the desk to pick something up. I'm gonna lock the door behind me, so you'll be perfectly safe, ma." I said lovingly while looking at her, sizing her thick ass up.

"I'll be here when you get back," she cracked and smiled, barely looking at me as she finished stocking the shelf she was working on.

I fully planned on making her ass pay for acting like her ass wasn't as turned the fuck on as I was…and gave her a warning.

"You gonna pay for that," I threw over my shoulder as I walked away.

"What I do – and do you promise?" she asked in a sexy ass voice that made my dick jump and I wasn't even looking in her direction.

"You'll see."

As soon as I got to the desk, the desk sergeant handed me a large brown bag from a delicatessen without a word while she held the phone against her neck and shuffled paperwork. I was happy it went that way because this particular sergeant could talk her ass off. I mouthed a silent thank you and offered a nod, which she returned before I headed back to the library. When I got back, I saw Natifah struggling to push the last of the heavy carts that needed to be emptied and stored away in the back rooms.

"You independent women kill me sometimes," I said with a chuckle. "Take this and let me grab that. You heard the warden. Let me handle the heavy lifting."

"I got something heavy you can lift," she playfully taunted.

"See, I'm trying to be a gentleman and make sure my lady eats before I suck some of the fire out ya fine ass. But you keep this up, your lunch will have to wait."

"Or I could eat my dick for lunch and have the actual food for dessert. What do you think, Officer Pratt?" she asked, giving me bedroom eyes.

"Whatever the lady wants."

"The lady wants her man to fuck her good and long – after…" she began dropping to her knees when we were in the back storage room. "I feel this thick, warm, veiny dick in the back of my throat."

"What the… fuuuuuuck…" I squawked – unable to say anything else before she started licking the length of my shaft. "Sssssss." I couldn't help but hiss.

"Mmmm…" she crooned as her head moved back and forth on my shaft.

Looking down, seeing my dick disappear between her pouty lips before reemerging glistening with her saliva, had my dick throbbing. She must've felt me looking down at her, because she gazed up at me with her almond eyes, making eye contact, which almost did a nigga in.

"What the… fuuuuuuuck." I grunted as I felt her tongue

massaging my seeds from my sack that fuckin' quick. "Daddy needs a taste. Get up, my love." I requested before taking her hand to help her to her feet.

Lifting her onto the desk that was now in the smaller storage area, I laid her back on the desk before relieving her of her bottoms and panties in one quick motion. Raising her knees and parting her thighs, my tongue left my lips on autopilot, anxious to make contact with her taut pearl.

"Mmmm…. Daddy," she wailed softly as I began my clitoral assault.

Her hands gently roamed my head as I used the tip of my tongue to tantalize her taut nub, before I had to wrap my lips around that sexy mufucka and apply some pressure. Her back arched wildly as I did that, and the leg I allowed to fall began to shake as her first orgasm approached.

"That's right, beautiful. Cum for big daddy." I roused before reattaching my mouth to her already creaming center.

"It's…. Ooooou, daddy… I… I can't…" she moaned breathily as she tried to keep to a whisper.

"Yes, you can, love. Daddy's thirsty. Let me drink." I commanded, and on cue, I felt her juices lightly splash my face and hit the back of my throat.

Her body fell limp to the desk as she panted. I could tell by the way her hands roamed her body and her legs were rubbing together like a cricket that her body was on fire. I stroked all her dick, making sure I was at a nice full erection before I pulled her sexy ass to the end of the desk and filled her to the hilt.

"God, I love this…. dick…" she confessed with her eyes closed as she took my strokes like a good girl.

"Because you love big daddy. Ain't that right?" I asked as I steadily moved in and out of her, watching her juicy pink walls cling to my dick with every stroke.

"With all my heart," was her reply.

"Sit up and look at me while I make you cum." I ordered, pulling her towards me before she could respond.

With the desk being the perfect height, I pulled her a little closer to the edge, she wrapped her legs around me, and I went to pound town on that pussy. She was doing good maintaining eye contact as we jockeyed for control. That was until that impending orgasm got to feeling too good and her eyes rolled back in her head.

"Nah uh. Eyes on Daddy, beautiful. Cum with me." I insisted. "Can big daddy cum with you?" I asked as I grabbed her ass cheeks and delivered deep powerful strokes to her core. "Huh?"

"Yes… Daddy…" she moaned softly as I felt her walls tighten the stranglehold it had on my dick, letting me know she was cumming.

"I ain't hear you right."

"Yes, daddy. Uuuuuuuugh!" she groaned lowly as I could see the fire leave her body through her eyes as she creamed all over my muscles.

"Fuuuuuck! I'm…cummin' too, ma. Grrrrrrr!" I roared with my face buried in her shoulder, filling her with my seeds as she held me.

"That was…" she began but paused to catch her breath.

"More amazing than usual. With yo ol' good pussy having, 'bout to be free, sexy ass." I said with a smile before kissing her and leaving her body.

"What you said, she agreed as I helped her off the desk. "And it's only gonna get more amazing."

"I like the way that sounds." I returned with a grin.

"You know what else I'd like?"

"What's that, ma?"

"Food. You done drained me of all my energy…big daddy."

"That's my name – and don't you forget that shit."

"I love your crazy ass," she said with a chuckle.

"I love your crazy ass right back."

Needless to say, although our bodily fluids were probably splashed amongst damn near every book in the library – which no one was none the wiser about – the state board members were more than happy with the library renovation. The warden's old, wrinkled ass beamed as he'd personally undertaken the task of the renovation himself; but I gave him his props for giving Natifah the much-deserved credit – because she did the damn thing. One of the board members even recommended that Natifah be kept as the prison librarian, which surprised me. But what surprised me even more was when his reply was:

"If only. Fortunately, for Ms. Foxworth here – but unfortunate for us here – this weekend will be her *last* behind these here walls. So, I think it's only fitting that we wish her the best with all her future endeavors, **outside** these walls."

I walked through the employee entrance door, cleared the checkpoint, and looked at my schedule for the week. In the library again. It'd been over a week since I'd seen or heard from Natifah, which was the day the state came for their walk-through. After they'd concluded their business in the library, the warden gave the okay for the library to stay close to the inmates for the rest of the day – as long as we agreed to make it look like we were doing work. We had to put on for surveillance of course, and as soon as the coast was clear, we put on for our own damn selves. Not only was it illegal for me to have an inmate cummin' all over used books and furniture, but the nasty shit we did to each other should have been illegal as well. Just thinking about it made my dick jump, even with me being a little pissed. Thinking about that day, and the way we made angry love to each other in that room, made me wonder if she fucked me the way she did as a goodbye. Just thinking about it made my otherwise tough-ass man heart hurt, and you know what they say, *hurt people, hurt people*. My saving grace was that it was Friday. So, I had the weekend to pull my shit together – after seemingly being thrown off my square by what I thought was true love.

When I got to the door of the library to open, Inmate Bates was waiting outside of the door. I bid her a good morning before she handed me her work slip. I was as polite as I could be while taking it from her and opening the door before leading the way inside. Asking her to just relax for a few minutes while I dropped off my things and started my shift reports, I returned to point out a few things that would be part of her work duties. I wanted to get that shit done and out of the way so I could return to the hub to find something… anything to take my mind off of Natifah. Something that was easier said than done, when her delicate hands had touched damn near everything in this space, and every corner held a memory of our time together.

Once lunchtime rolled around, I heard a knock at the hub door. Looking up from my reports to see it was Bates, I waved her inside.

"W'sup, Baines?" I asked kindly but in a nonchalant tone.

"Am I clear for the mess hall?" she asked with a slight smile.

"Oh, yeah. It is about that time." I replied while glancing at the cheap, metal grate-covered clock on the wall. "I'd say enjoy, but we both know how that goes." I offered – too nice of a guy to take my frustrations out on her.

"I second that," she returned with a chuckle. "See you in thirty."

"I've been meaning to ask about the research for your appeal that Foxworth was helping you out with. How's that coming along?"

"It's going great. I'm getting a new trial. I swear that girl is a genius," she informed with a smile. "I wish I had a chance to thank her before she left. I don't think I would've gotten a new trial without her."

"Well, I'm sure she knows you appreciated her help." I tried to hide how much I missed her. "Congratulations to you though. I hope everything works out in your best interest." I added, sincerely.

"Thank you, Officer Pratt. I appreciate that and your help as well."

"I'm glad I could pitch in, even if it was just a little something." I offered with a smile, ready for the conversation to be over so I could be alone with my turkey salad sandwich and my thoughts. "Well, enjoy. See you back here after chow."

I turned my focus back to the computer screen, letting her

know our conversation was over. The way she lingered in the doorway let me know she had something else she possibly wanted to say, but I wasn't interested. There was only one woman on my mind and heart that I wanted to talk to – and her ass damn sure wasn't her.

Once my reports were done, I unpacked my lunch, pulled out my cell, and decided to search social media to see if I could track Natifah down. I swear it was like searching for Cinderella with only a glass slipper to work with. When I came across her social media pages, seeing her face made my heart smile, but that shit turned upside down when I saw they had not been updated. There were no new pictures, or status updates… zip. I was running into dead end after dead end, which was only frustrating me further, so I gave up.

"I guess it was too good to be true," I said aloud as I logged out of my social media with a sigh. "Fuck love."

WHEN I PULLED into the driveway of my crib, I already had the rest of my night planned out. It was straight to the showers – as usual – a cold beer, and I was hitting the fellas up to see what was poppin' for the night. I'd be damned if I was gonna sit in the crib all up in my feelings, playing with my dick. I had a woman that was supposed to be doing that. Or so I thought. But with the situation being what it was, all a brotha could do was adapt to the circumstances.

I was just finalizing plans with my boy Rashun when my doorbell rang. I never had anyone to just show up at my crib, unless it was my mom or one of the fellas, and I wasn't expecting either. Looking at the camera on my phone, I was a little puzzled at the figure I saw on my porch. It was a woman, and she had her back turned towards the camera. It was cold as Frosty's ass crack out, so the North Face coat with the fur-rimmed hood wasn't out of place. Still, I needed to know who the fuck it was, and more importantly, how the fuck did they find out where I lived?

"Can I help you with something?" I asked, sternly.

When she heard my voice over the speaker, I could see her body tense. I could see her chest rise and fall as if she was preparing herself to do or say something – but I wasn't in the mood, and the shit was taking too long.

"I suggest you say something or move along please," I said through the speaker.

"I um… I'm not sure if I'm at the right place, and I know I shouldn't have come unannounced, but I'm looking for Jabril Pratt," she announced, finally facing the camera, but she stood too close for me to make out her face under the hood.

I knew I probably should've asked more questions, especially since all I was wearing was a towel, but on autopilot, I grabbed my pistol and made my way to the door. When I cracked it open, I didn't recognize the face that stared back at me, but somehow, she looked familiar.

"Oh my," she blushed.

"Oh shit. My bad. Excuse me one minute." I rushed out. Especially after that cold air hit my almost naked body.

I partially closed the door and grabbed a terrycloth robe that I kept on the coat rack that my mom had given me one year for Christmas. Once I was suitable, I re-opened the door and started my question.

"So, who did you say you were?" I asked, knowing she never did.

"My name is Nadia. You don't know me, but I damn sure feel like I know you already," she beamed.

"Ooookay. I'm um…a little confused. I know you how?" I enquired, still puzzled, but for whatever reason, very intrigued.

"Boy! Is you Jabril or what? It's cold out this bitch," she sassed, placing a hand on her hip.

"I'll be damned if your attitude doesn't remind me of someone I know…very well," I replied and dropped my head as I chuckled, thinking again of Natifah. "To answer your question, yes…I'm Jabril."

"Good… and I probably remind you of that bitch because I'm her sister. Her punk ass wanted to send me out in the cold to make sure we had the right spot because she was scared," she fussed. "Stalker much? Not that I blame her. You are type fine."

"Uh…thanks," was my reply as I chuckled again. "Is she…"

"Bitch…. this the right house. Bring your ass so I can go pick up these badass kids!" she yelled from the porch before turning her attention back to me. "It was nice meeting you, but I gotta go. I got a babysitter for maybe one more hour, and I'm trying to get a quickie in before them crumb snatchers invade. You'll get my meaning soon. Anyway, I'll interrogate you a little more properly later, but it was lovely meeting you," she rushed out before turning to walk down my porch steps.

As she stepped down my porch steps, I looked up just as the passenger door of the Audi she drove opened. Another white North Face-clad body with fur trim emerged from the car. The two embraced before the other figure moved toward me. When they lifted their head, the hood fell off, confirming it was indeed *her*. Simultaneously, my heart began to beat again.

"Hey, big daddy," she greeted before smiling brightly.

"Oh my… Bring your ass here, girl!" I emitted, rushing outside, forgetting that I was only wearing a robe and slippers. It was twenty-five degrees outside, and snow covered the ground. "Shit, it's cold."

"Can I come inside – or is your woman at home?" she asked with a smirk.

"I thought she left me and my dick with a broken heart, but she's

home now." I corrected while stepping aside before we both entered my house.

"Never that – and yes, mama's home," she confirmed.

Seeing her outside of the library was like seeing her in a whole new light. She was even more beautiful than the last time I'd seen her, and it'd only been a week. I had so many questions and emotions running through me, but none of that mattered. I just wanted to touch her. Feel her. Be with her. So, that's what went down. We kissed each other with more hunger and lust than I'd ever felt as I rushed to free her body from her coat. The tights and tunic sweater fit her curvy body perfectly. A body I couldn't wait to see fully naked, standing in front of me.

We separated our lips long enough for me to pull her sweater over her head, and then my lips were attached to her neck and breasts as I backed her further into the living room. Pausing to relieve myself of my robe and towel, I laid her gently on the couch before gently hovering over her.

"I love you so much, beautiful. I thought I'd lost you," were the sincere words that left my lips.

"You'll never lose me. I love you too much. There's been…" she began, but I silenced her with a finger over her lips before replacing it with mine.

The prison-issued panties I'd only ever seen her in used to drive me crazy, so the sexy lace thongs she now wore had my head ready to pop off. As she lay beneath me naked, I took a quick moment to take her in, in all her naked glory before I began devouring her. She no longer had to quiet her moans as I sucked and licked on the left nipple, before moving onto the right. When they were nice and hard, standing at attention like perfect little gumdrops, I kissed everywhere there was skin from those big ol titties to big daddy's juicy pussy. I spread her thick, mocha thighs as she liked to call them, and smiled when the entryway to my heaven stared me in the face. Licking my lips, I gave her a devilish grin before attaching the lips on my face to her plump, freshly waxed lips.

"Oooou… God, I missed you…" she moaned sexily as her hands began to gently roam my low-cut waves.

"I missed you more," I mumbled back, refusing to tear my lips away from her pussy.

I didn't know if it was because I had been missing the hell outta her ass or what, but the pussy was wetter. Sweeter. Juicier than it had ever been. I wrapped my legs around her thighs and went in like a national pie-eating contest was on the line. She was still containing her moans, but we ain't have to do that shit no more, and I reminded her of that.

"Let that shit out, beautiful," I stated with a slap on the side of her plump ass. "Sound off for Big Daddy the way you've always wanted to."

"Thank… God! Yasss… big daddy!" she screamed as I admired her full breasts rising and falling as she panted.

Come to find out, my baby was not only a creamer but a screamer – and I didn't know if I mentioned previously that she was a squirter too. Anyway, once I sucked the soul outta her sexy ass, I wasted no time filling her slick walls. Placing a leg on my shoulders, I kissed up to her toes as I ground deep into her center. Her walls welcomed Daddy back home, and daddy was damn sure cuttin' up in his pussy.

"Come ride your dick, beautiful," I told her before leaving her body and offering a hand to help her up. I needed to see her sexy ass move on top of me.

Natifah straddled my lap and lowered herself onto my dick as my hands found their way to her hips. Looking into my eyes first, she kissed me deeply as she began to rock her hips slowly. My baby went straight rude gyal on me with all the winding and gyrating she was doing on this dick. There were no work boots to hide my toes from curling. My shits were throwing up fraternity letters, gang signs, pop lockin'. At one point, I didn't know whose moans were louder. What I did know was that shit didn't matter, because as we both approached our climax, only moans and skin slapping could be heard.

"What the…. fuuuuuuuck?!" I groaned out as I felt my nut rise from my toes.

"I'm cummin', daddy. Ooooou shit! Oooooooooou!" she moaned and did the cutest giggle thing before she yelled out, "Dadddddyyyyyyy!" as she came harder than I'd ever seen, with me right behind her.

Natifah was still sitting atop me as we both sat quietly, catching our breaths as we held each other. Hands roamed damp skin as we just enjoyed the afterglow. The silence. Each other.

"Woman… I don't know about you, but I think you

might've gotten me pregnant… and the way you work that thang, you ain't shooting no blanks." I cracked and chuckled.

"Neither are you," was her reply as she slowly lifted her head and looked into my eyes.

"Hell nah! My soldiers are strong like bulls. Shiiid, I'm surprised you're not…" I began and stopped when she raised a perfectly arched eyebrow. "Wait. So, you… Are you…?" I stammered.

"I am," she replied and moved to get off my lap.

"Nah. Where are you going?" I asked, holding her tighter to keep her from moving. "And what's with that look?"

"Jabril, this… isn't something either of us expected. So, I would understand if this baby, or this relationship for that matter, is something you've changed your mind about."

"Changed my mind about?" I asked, looking at her like she had two heads. "Baby, it's only been a week since I've last touched you, and a nigga was losing his shit. I been on your social media pages. I was about to be on some Arnold in the *Terminator* type shit and find me a phone book to track your ass down listing by listing. You are *the best* thing that's ever happened to me, and this baby is going to be a very close second. I could never change my mind about you. I love you."

"I love you more, baby. I just want us to work. To last. To do this right; and if I'm right, we have everything we need if we put in the work," she said with a cute ass smile as she gently stroked my face.

"Shiiid, I was just puttin' in hella work. I ain't gonna

front…you were putting in work too. About to have a nigga bitch up. Get all Carl Thomas' 'Emotional'." I cracked.

"You so damn nasty," she spat and slapped my shoulder before she laughed.

"And yo ass is too. That's why you're pregnant now." I boasted. "My ass is about to be a dad yo! I knew them titties were looking extra right and how wet you are. Wow!" I screamed.

"Yeah. Imagine my surprise when I went in for a routine checkup and found out I came home from prison with a little more than some memories and a souvenir," she cracked and chuckled. "I have no regrets though. I'm a better woman because of it, and some of that, my love, is because of you," she added before kissing my forehead. And that was it for me. The 'Soul' kiss.

"Natifah. I know this shit probably sounds crazy as hell, but I've never been more sure of anything in my life. I want you to answer honestly. Not with your head, but with your heart. Agreed?" I asked excitedly.

"Agreed."

"Cool. So, it's like this. Your ass ain't going anywhere… ever, and neither am I. We gonna put in this work, be good to each other, and raise a super smart-ass kid. Our shit is gonna be old-school Tupperware tight. So, I'm begging you…. Will you please be my wife?" I proposed, looking into her eyes for the answer I needed to hear.

"Hell yeah."

"Cool. Now get off me so we can shower and get dressed." I said, excited as hell and damn near pushing her off me. When I moved to get up, my cell began to ring.

"Well damn," she squealed, throwing a pillow at me as she laughed. "Where are we going, crazy man?"

"I'mma answer that in one second," I replied as I answered the call. "W'sup, Shun?" I asked, placing him on speaker.

"W'sup is we on our way to come pick your sensitive ass up so we can turn the fuck up. That's w'sup, nigga!" he yelled loudly into the phone.

Looking at Natifah, I handed her the phone as I grabbed my laptop and got busy.

"Hey, fellas. Unfortunately, Jabril's plans have changed, and his sensitive ass is turning up with me tonight. We're about to shower and go to… Where are we going, Daddy?"

"She calls this nigga *daddy*?" Shun asked in disbelief over the phone, earning a slight chuckle from her.

"Big daddy to be exact, my nigga. But I'mma catch up with y'all in a couple of days. We are bout to go hop on this flight to Vegas and jump the broom. I'll holla!"

THE END

Did you enjoy the read?

Let us know how much by leaving us a review on Amazon and Goodreads.

Keep reading for a preview of…

The State's Witness: An Unwanted Dilemma

By Kyiris Ashley

CHAPTER 1

Russell laid back in bed with his legs spread as he looked up at the ceiling. Tianna sat between them with his manhood in her mouth. However, she was taking way too long to make him nut. She didn't know how to suck dick at all, and he knew he would have to give her several lessons before she would be decent at it. In all of his twenty-eight years of life, he'd never had to teach a woman how to suck dick, but for Tianna, he would do so. He liked her vibe and wanted to keep her around. Russell focused his dark brown eyes on the porn that was being played on the fifty-five-inch television in front of him. He bit his bottom lip as he watched the thick, brown skinned woman get pounded from behind. Closing his eyes, he focused on the woman's moans and his dick hardened. Placing his hand on the back of Tianna's head, he pushed it down, causing his dick to go deeper down her throat.

Tianna gagged, forcing more saliva to enter her mouth. Russell grabbed one of her nipples and twirled it between his fingers as he held her head in place. With his eyes still closed, Russell's toes curled as he sensed the feeling of his climax nearing.

"Yes bitch, suck that dick for daddy. Get all that nut outta there," Russell panted, just as he released his warm cum down Tianna's throat.

Tianna sat up and wiped her mouth with her hand. She looked at the way Russell was laid out and breathing heavy, and a smile crossed her face.

"Did I do good, baby?" She asked, eager to hear his answer.

Russell had told her on several occasions that she didn't know how to perform oral sex. She knew that was something Russell really liked, and in order to keep him happy, she wanted to learn the ends and outs. So, she watched porn and searched Goggle in an effort to master the skill of giving head.

"Yeah, that was pretty dope. I'm glad no teeth came out this time. You still have some work to do but you are getting' better," Russell replied.

In reality, Russell wouldn't have came if it wasn't for the porn. He just didn't want to hurt Tianna's pride. He could tell that she really wanted to please him, so he just let her think she had done so.

"I'm gonna get in the shower, I have to work in the

mornin'. Are you spendin' the night tonight?" Tianna asked as she stood from the bed.

"Nah, not to night, my baby."

Russell saw the change in Tianna's demeanor and knew she wanted him to stay, but he had money to collect. It was always money over bitches in his eyes. Tianna wasn't making him any money, so he wasn't about to keep wasting his time with her.

"How much you makin' at that little job you got?" Russell asked as he zipped his pants.

"Bout seven hundred every two weeks," Tianna answered confidently.

"What if I tell you I know a way you can double that in just one week, maybe even a few days, dependin' on how good you work?"

"I'm listenin'," Tianna replied.

"You gotta use what you got to get what you want. Has anybody ever told you that as long as you got a pussy, you should never be broke?"

Tianna looked at Russell perplexed. Did this dude just call me broke? I had just swallowed his kids while he moaned like a little bitch, and he has the nerve to stand here and insult me? I may not be big ballin', but I was definitely livin' comfortably. Tianna thought, quickly becoming irritated by the way Russell was talking to her.

"No disrespect, my baby, I'm just tryin' to put you up on game. Let's be real, you been fuckin' and suckin' on me for the last six weeks, for free. I'm sure it's a dozen other niggas that can say that too."

"Are you suggesting that I should fuck for money?" Tianna asked, damn near ready to slap the shit out of Russell.

"Hell yeah, you been givin' it out for free this long. You might as well put a price on that muthafucka."

Russell reached into his pocket and pulled out a wad of money and held it up in Tianna's face, showing her all the bills. He watched as her eyes got wide, and he knew he'd just reeled her in.

"You see this? I made this shit in one week, spreading my knowledge and taking care of girls just like you. You could be makin' this too, just by layin' on yo back or getting' on yo knees. You young and tight, niggas will pay big money for you."

Tianna thought for a minute as she stared at the money in Russell's hand. Money signs started invading her mind, as she thought about all the new things she could buy with the fast money. This could possibly be the lick she was looking for that could change her life forever.

"So, how much you think I can make?" She asked quickly, eagerness in her tone.

Russell looked at her tight, shapely body and short, blonde pixie cut. Tianna stood about five two, with thick hips and ass, and perfect perky C cup breasts. At eighteen with no kids, her body was perfect, and Russell knew the niggas would pay big for her. Although she was black, her butter pecan colored skin and hazel eyes gave her an exotic look, and he knew he could sale that.

"About twelve hundred a week," he replied.

That was a lot of money. Tianna started to do the math in her head. She figured if she worked with Russell for a year, she would be able to purchase her clothing store and become her own boss. It had been her dream for as long as Tianna could remember to own her own boutique. She knew it would take years to save up for it working at McDonald's. She could save for a decade and still not have enough with the pennies she made there.

"When can I start?" Tianna asked.

Russell smiled because that hadn't taken nearly as much convincing as he thought it would. It was almost too easy, like taking candy from a baby.

"Don't go to work in the mornin'. I'll be back over here in a few hours and we can take some pictures of you to post on my site. After I post them, you should be getting' to work within an hour. That shit don't take long at all."

Tianna nodded her head in understanding, eager to see how the money would start rolling in. She'd never thought she would be selling sex on the internet, but there was no way Tianna could pass up that type of money. Tianna would damn near sale her soul to make enough money to start her own business. Although she didn't realize it, in a way, she was.

"Get you some rest, my baby, you gonna need it, cuz it's gonna be a long night. And that shit smell like money," Russell said, rubbing his hands together while smiling.

Russell walked out the door and Tianna got in bed. She set her alarm for midnight, knowing that Russell would be returning around that time. She fell asleep with money on her mind, feeling as though her hustle was just about to begin.

When her clock alarmed at midnight, Tianna rushed to get into the shower. She knew Russell was on his way, and she didn't want to keep him waiting. She quickly showered and rubbed shea butter all over her body before putting on her robe. There was a knock on the door, and she rushed to it, knowing exactly who it was.

"I brought you somethin' sexy to take pictures in," Russell announced. Holding up a red lace pantie and bra set.

Tianna took the lingerie from his hand and went to the bathroom to put them on. She looked at herself in the mirror and knew that a red lip and a set of false lashes would set the look off. She made her way to her vanity and took a seat, ready to complete the look. When she walked back out to the living room with Russell, he smiled at her beauty. Standing to his feet, he removed his phone from his pocket.

Tianna posed several different ways as Russell snapped shot after shot. Russell directed her on different sexier poses for him to snap, telling her to lean against the couch with her leg up. Or squat down with her legs spread and her tongue out. Tianna obliged without protest, doing everything Russell said. When they were done, he picked her four best pictures to post. No sooner than Tianna changed out of the lingerie did Russell tell her she had a date.

"He wants head and pussy, and you gonna make one fifty off the deal," Russell informed.

"Cool, where is this going down at?" Tianna asked.

"We gonna meet him at a room. Go get changed and put on something sexy. Meet me at my truck when you done," Russell spoke, grabbing his keys from Tianna's coffee table.

When they made it to the motel, Russell told Tianna to stay in the car while he went and collected the money. Russell had a strict policy and let all the men know that nothing went down until all the money was in his hand. The man opened the room door and Russell stepped inside. He looked around the room, and in the bathroom, making sure nobody else was inside the room. Russell had only given the john the price for one person and wanted to make sure he wasn't getting played. Once he was sure no one else other than the man was inside, Russell collected four hundred and fifty dollars from him, then walked back out to the car.

"He's ready for you," Russell stated, and Tianna got out of the car.

She walked up to the motel room door and smiled when she saw the man standing on the other side. He was a tall white man who seemed to be in his mid to late forties. He was handsome, with dark brown hair and brown eyes. She could tell he worked out by his washboard stomach. She was happy that he wasn't ugly and fat.

"Hello there," Tianna greeted, as she closed the door behind her.

"Wow, you are absolutely beautiful. What is your name?" He asked.

Tianna though for a moment, cussing herself for not thinking of a name before she got there. Knowing she wasn't going to give her government name; she said the first thing that came to mind.

"You can call me Amber," Tianna replied, as she walked closer to the man.

She slowly began unbuttoning his shirt, revealing his carved chest. Once his shirt was off, she unbuckled his belt and allowed his pants to drop to the floor. She could see his erect manhood standing at attention through his black silk boxers. Tianna was just about to pull them down when he stopped her.

"I paid for you, so let me do this how I want to," He whispered.

Tianna obliged and allowed the man to take control. He pulled Tianna's tight black dress off her and revealed her naked body. The man licked his lips as he stared at Tianna. Bringing her over to the bed, he laid her down and buried his face between her thick thighs. Tianna moaned as the man's wet tongue gave her more pleasure than she'd ever had. When he was done, he placed a condom on his penis and climbed on top of her. Tianna moaned as he entered her.

For this to be her first time on the job, she was really enjoying this. She wasn't nervous at all like she thought she would be. If every time could be just like this, Tianna was going to love her job. Tianna threw it back and popped her pussy like she had known this man for years. When they were done, Tianna was spent. Naked, she walked into the bathroom to wash the sex from her body. When she returned to the room, her john was already fully dressed and sitting on the bed they had just fucked in.

"Here you go, this is for you," he said, handing her two-hundred-dollar bills.

"Oh, I thought you already paid Russell," Tianna said, confused.

"I did, but I really enjoyed myself with you, so this is your tip," he replied with a wink.

Tianna smiled and placed the money in her bra before thanking him. There was no way she was going to tell Russell about the extra money she'd received. Tianna walked out the room and back to the car with Russell. That's when he informed her that she had another date at the hotel down the street. Tianna smiled and nodded her head as Russell pulled out the parking lot.

Available Now On All Platforms

ALSO BY TAMYRA GRIFFIN

The Point of It All

The Point of It All 2

The Point of It All 3

The Point of It All 4

The Point of It All 5

Daddy's Princess, His Rider

Money Makin Mama

Money Makin Mama 2

Bitter Heart: A Lover Scorn

Blood Ties & Lies

Pregnant By My Husband's Father

Pregnant By My Husband's Father 2

My Fairyhood Romance

Me, Myself, and Iyana

Sugah Cookies: A Christmas Erotica

Delicious: A BBW Romance

Sauce: When She Is The Plug

*Never Tell A B*tch Your Business*

Ex-Factor: When Leaving Someone Who Refuses To Let Go

Unpretty

Only Death Can Keep Me From Him

*Ashes To Ashes To A Broke B*tch*

OTHER BOOKS BY

URBAN AINT DEAD

Tales 4rm Da Dale

The Hottest Summer Ever

Hittin' Licks For The Holidays: Atlanta

Wet Dreams On Lockdown: The Nurse

By **Elijah R. Freeman**

Despite The Odds

By **Juhnell Morgan**

Good Girl Gone Rogue

By **Manny Black**

Hittaz

Hittaz 2

Hittaz 3

Hittaz 4

Coldhearted

By **Lou Garden Price, Sr.**

Charge It To The Game

Charge It To The Game 2

A Summer To Remember With My Hitta

Snatched Up By A Hitta

Santa Sent Me A Real One For Christmas

Wet Dreams on Lockdown: The Unit Manager

By **Nai**

A Setup For Revenge

Wet Dreams On Lockdown: Librarian

By **Ashley Williams**

Ridin' For You

Trickin' on a Heaux for Christmas: A BBW Love Story

Homie Hoppin' For The Holidays

By **Telia Teanna**

The State's Witness

The State's Witness 2

The State's Witness 3

By **Kyiris Ashley**

Stuck In The Trenches

Stuck In The Trenches 2

By **Huff Tha Great**

The Swipe

By **Toōla**

Melted the Heart of a Menace

By P. Wise

Merry Trapmas: Ice & Frost

By **Mia Sky**

Thug Me The Right Way

By **DiamondATL & Nai**

Ridin For You, Too
Wet Dreams On Lockdown: The Female C.O
By **Telia Teanna**

A Setup For Revenge 2
By **Ashley Williams**

A Gangsta's Last Kiss
By **Mia Sky**

Pretti & The Beast
Wet Dreams On Lockdown: Lieutenant Grace
By **P. Wise**

Wet Dreams On Lockdown: The Counselor
By **Paris Iman**

Wet Dreams On Lockdown: The Captain
By **TN Jones**

Wet Dreams On Lockdown: The Warden
By **Shawnice**

BOOKS BY

URBAN AINT DEAD's C.E.O

<u>Elijah R. Freeman</u>

Triggadale

Triggadale 2

Triggadale 3

Tales 4rm Da Dale

The Hottest Summer Ever

Murda Was The Case

Murda Was The Case 2

Murda Was The Case 3

Hittin' Licks For The Holidays: Atlanta

Wet Dreams On Lockdown: The Nurse

www.ingramcontent.com/pod-product-compliance
Lightning Source LLC
Chambersburg PA
CBHW071157300726
48975CB00004B/1187